Budham Sharanam

Budham Sharanam

Namrata Chadha

Translated by
Dr. Nidhi Garg

BLACK EAGLE BOOKS
Dublin, USA | BBSR, India

Black Eagle Books
USA address:
7464 Wisdom Lane
Dublin, OH 43016

India address:
E/312, Trident Galaxy, Kalinga Nagar,
Bhubaneswar-751003, Odisha, India

E-mail: info@blackeaglebooks.org
Website: www.blackeaglebooks.org

First International Edition Published by
Black Eagle Books, 2022

BUDHAM SHARANAM
by **Namrata Chadha**
Translated by **Dr. Nidhi Garg**

Original Copyright © Namrata Chadha
Translation Copyright © Dr. Nidhi Garg

Cover : **Umasankar Bhuyan**
Interior Design: Ezy's Publication

ISBN- 978-1-64560-087-9 (Paperback)
Library of Congress Control Number: 2022950386

Printed in the United States of America

Dedicated to
Triple Gem
&
Kapish-Kanishk-Kabir

Biswa Bhusan Harichandan

RAJ BHAVAN
VIJAYAWADA-520002

GOVERNOR
ANDHRA PRADESH

PREFACE

Written by Mrs. Namrata Chaddha, this book contains a collection of stories of women whose lives became difficult during the Buddhist period. There are a total of 17 short stories in the book, out of which 15 have been written about women of the Buddhist period, who, influenced by the Buddhist philosophy of God, made their own life and found a way to be free from inequality. The original mantra was 'budham sharanam gachami, sangham sharanam gachami'. This book can be useful for society in the era of all the efforts of women's empowerment. This is a document of women's discussion in the Buddhist period, which has been interestingly presented to the readers. This collection of short stories is not only brief but also interesting and linguistically easy to read. After the establishment of the Buddhist Sangha for the monks, a separate establishment of the Bhikkhuni Sangha is also said to have probably taken place in Vaishali. The core of his teachings was Sangham Sharanam Gachhami. It is said that when Buddha returned to Kapilvastu, he saw the same urge to join the sangha of the Shakya women as there was in the men. However, his Kshirdayika Mata (maternal aunt) Gautami had asked him for permission to enter the union of women, which the Buddha refused. Women eager to enter the Sangh, including Gautami, changed their dresses. Just like monks, they shaved their hair and wore clothes. Gautami talked to Ananda, the disciple of Buddha, about this. On his request, women entered the Sangh. Tathagata

(Buddha) also told his disciple Ananda that he knew that women can attain Nirvana like men. He does not consider men special than women. His disagreement with the entry of women into the Sangh was for practical reasons. Lord Buddha asked women to accept eight things in order to be permitted into the Sangha. These are called Athaguru Dhamma (Eight Guru Dharma). In the first group, eight hundred women joined the Buddhist Sangha. Among them was Yashodhara. Mallika, Ksemavati, Amrapali, Prakriti, Khujutra etc. are those women who, in the time about two and a half thousand years ago, when women were considered far below men, they were forced to live under the umbrella of their husbands or son, in a male-dominated society, women had to follow the set standards, in such an environment the issue of women's rights, women's equality was strongly raised. It is believed that the Buddha was concerned about the difficulties caused by the entry of women. That is why a separate Sangh was established in Vaishali. Its details are available in Therigatha. Many women started entering the Sangh as soon as their husbands joined the Sangh. Most of them were unhappy, bereaved of children and due to other social reasons used to enter the Sangh. Women of all classes got admitted into the bhikkhuni sangha. These nuns have been looked upon with respect. This tradition is still there today. Like the Bhikshu Sangha, the contribution of the Bhikkhuni Sangha is no less in the propagation of Indian culture, especially the Buddha discourses.

It would be fair to say that in this book of Namrata ji, the stories of women of the Buddhist period are interesting in themselves, whose brief descriptions will be readable. The book gives the message that taking refuge in religion and God is the only way to attain salvation. Lord Buddha paved the way for women's upliftment and equal rights in the male society which considered women as objects of enjoyment and dependence. This can be said to be a compassionate struggle of women in the Buddhist period. I wish the success of this book of Namrata ji.

(Shri Vishwabhushan Harichandan)

NAMO BUDDHAYA

MAHA BODHI SOCIETY OF INDIA

(Premier International Buddhist Organisation : Estd.-1891)
Founder : Bodhisatthva Anagarika Dharmapala
[Registered under W.B.S.R. Act, 1961-Regn. No. 2666 of 1915-16]
Visit us : www.mbsiindia.org

1864 – 1933

19th November, 2020

MESSAGE

    The women are the mothers and nourishers for the mankind, but they have been put to suffer through social and gender discriminations throughout the ages. Women were barred to take part on social platforms and in religious rituals. Gautam Buddha was the first to open the doors to religious dignity and spiritual salvation for them. The most significant and revolutionary step was the establishment of the Bhikkhuni or Nuns Order in Buddhism. With this right of entering and treading on the path of the Buddha and also guiding others to the achievement of Nibbana – the highest bliss, the women came to same status as of men. The movement of 'Women's Empowerment' thus got initiated from the time of Buddha. The teachings of the Buddha are relevant and good solution of many social issues of all the times.

    The book – "Buddham Saranam", written by Ms. Namrata Chaddha, a Senior Member of Maha Bodhi Society of India, will act as great inspiration for all women going forth on the way of social, religious and spiritual upliftment.

    Bhavatu Sabba Mangalam,

(Ven. P. Seewalee Thero)
General Secretary,
Maha Bodhi Society of India

SILA   Samadhi   Pragya

DHAMMA SOCIETY INDIA

Nand Niketan, Naka Hindola, Lucknow (INDIA)
Regd. No. 2734-2007-2008 Dt. 18.03.2008

Mahendra Singh 'Buddhaputta'
Former Special Secretary, U.P. Govt.
Chairman-Dhamma Society India

Flat No. : 3002, Heritage Apartments,
5 Park Road, Lucknow-226001
Mob. : 07388755555/08009999990
Email : buddhaputtamsingh345@gmail.com

Since I met Namrata Chadha and heard her views which were found quite lucid, upright, just, replete with human values and egality. She is the champion to give a clarion call candidly without any fear or hesitation. May it be the cause of woman-child atrocity, injustice with down-trodden, have-nots or any type of social evil, she is found a front-runner to raise her voice for its redressal. She has set various mile-stones in litrary, legal, social and other fields. In a word, she is a multi-faceted pesonality.

But this time, Namrata Chadha has carved a niche in the dead wall to rekindle the Dhamma-Lamp of the Teaching of the Buddha by authoring a wonderful book under the caption "BUDDHAM SARNAM". This work illustrates the lives of certain 17 "Bhikkhunis" (Theries) of Buddha's period so naively. Her this work not only implies the advertence to socio-religious egalitarianism of Buddha to uplift the women to juxtapose them equal to the status of men, but certainly encourage and remind the present women-folk the role they played so magnificently in socio-religious front which used to be understood exclusive domain of the men. Perhaps this is the first ever attempt by any woman-author it is not the final. It is auspicious beginning never to end.

I think Namratha Chadha will not stop here but see will continue to right more and more on the lives of other Theries (Bhikkhunis) in a series to keep the Dhamma-lamp a flame to enlighten and awaken the society from the Deep sleep of ignorance. Dhamma danam sabba danam jinati (Dhamma dana excels all the dana).

I wish and bless her quite happy, healthy, prosperous and the longest course of life. May it be so.

Bhavatu Sabba Mangalam,
With highest Metta,

Dated:- 17-11-2020

M. Singh

(Mahendra Singh)

From writer's Pen

The original mantra Buddham Sharanam Gachhami Dhammam Sharanam Gachhami was the mantra of liberation from slavery for women of the Buddhist period. I have made a small effort to compile representative stories of women from the Buddhist period and present them in the form of a book. The purpose behind this was that the condition of women in that period was pathetic, they were considered an object of enjoyment. Along with being considered a luxury item, allegations like characterlessness and luxury were made against them. After a few years of attaining enlightenment, Lord Buddha did the work of giving equal status to women in society. Along with the monks, he established a separate sangha for nuns as well. The women whose stories are being presented in the life of Buddha through my book show that Lord Buddha was against patriarchal social values. He made a meaningful effort to make women equal to men in society. If said, the seed of women's empowerment was planted in the Buddhist period itself. When Buddha accepted the hospitality of the dancer Ambapali only then it was proved that he wanted to end inequality between men and women. It was this human aspect of the personality of Buddha's senior disciple, Ananda, who was deeply concerned about the condition of women, that he had convinced Buddha to include and rescue women in the Buddhist Sangha. The bhikkhus sangha was given higher status by dividing the sangha into separate categories of bhikkhus and bhikshuni. The role of bhikshus used to be relatively important in the propagation of Buddhism. Gradually bhikshunis were also trained and made capable of the same. Ten conditions or rules of bhikshuni were made, and only after following them could a woman become a bhikshuni. In the Buddhist legends, it was mentioned that some terms or conditions were to hurt the heart. No matter how senior the bhikkhuni may be, if any junior bhikkhu comes she will have to bow to him. That is, for the sake of respect, senior nuns had to bear this sting of humiliation. Not only this but if the bhikkhus and the bhikshunis made the same mistake, the bhikshunis were punished severely. No one opened his mouth on these monastic excesses. This means that the path of women's empowerment was open but the domination used to be of men only. All these things are mentioned in the Buddhist literature the way they were laid siege reminds them of the beliefs of Brahmin literature. It had become a tradition that women could be safe only under the protection of their husbands and son. Although this tradition is still more or less continued gradually the atmosphere is changing. It was beyond imagination even in the eyes of Buddha himself that a woman could be a Tathagata or a Chakravarti! Here the question may also be raised as to how Buddhism could have been liberal towards women by keeping women apart or deprived of participation in socio-religious life. The short stories written in the book show that women's upliftment started in the Buddhist period. The other thing is that the concept of women's empowerment or upliftment may not have been compatible with the framework. But from this, the generosity of Buddhism towards women cannot be denied. Our colleagues raised the question why are you compiling selected stories of the Buddhist period? I had to tell them that in today's era, the slogan of women empowerment to a greater extent has become a slogan for the fulfillment of political ambitions. The ground reality is something else. It is not that nothing has happened in the field of women's upliftment. A lot happened but its seed was planted in the Buddhist period. So far this movement is moving towards attainment even towards fulfillment but in a slow way. Even today male society is dominating. One of the objectives behind writing this book is to make the new generation aware of these stories which have become a document of social change. It is my authorship that from the very beginning I have been interested in Buddhism and Buddhist literature. While working on women's rights, often Buddhist women's stories used to go around the human psyche. There is a small attempt to make these scattered stories readable by storing them in the least number of words. I believe that the relevance of the teachings and philosophy of Lord Buddha will remain forever. As much as historians may have rarely mentioned the Buddhist period, the propagators of Buddhism got the iron of its relevance to the world. At the same time, I also want to say that whatever amount will be received in the form of royalty from the book will go to the account of the Mahabodhi Society so that it can be used in the teaching of Buddhism. And lastly, I would like to express my gratitude to Upasika Usha Buddh and Kajri Baruah who helped in gathering the material. Hafiza Begum and Manju Grover assembled the manuscript. Senior journalists Anjani Nigam and Mahesh Sharma assisted in editing. I am also grateful to Ven. Sourendra kumar Mahapatra Trustee of Maha Bodhi

Society of India for supporting the publication of this book. I am also thankful to Dr. Nidhi Garg for sincerely working on the translation of the book from Hindi to English with dedication and devotion. Had it not been for the cooperation of all of them, this book would not have been in your hand.

- **Namrata**

CONTENTS

Goutami 19

Yashodhara 32

Sujata 49

Khemavati 57

Kundalkeshi 66

Amrapali 77

Mallika 89

Utpalvarna 96

Krishna Gautami 106

Visakha 112

Chandalini 121

Patchara 130

Manvika Chincha 142

Khujjuttra 154

Datta 159

Sanghamitra 170

Kung's mother 180

Goutami

Nepal is blessed with nature, the peaks of the Himalayan mountains standing high all around, the rivers flowing, the lush green fields in the Terai areas and the unique forests, dwelled in small republics of the northern states on the western side of north India. These republics were often ruled by Kshatriya descendants. But in some remote hilly areas, it was the tribal natives who lived in small communities that ran their governance by their own policy rules.

The Terai region of Nepal was ruled by kings of the Colliery dynasty. King Anjandev had no children. He performed so many rituals, yajnas, havans, pujas and *archanas*. His queen Sulakshana was also eager to become a mother. She worshipped the nature goddess that destroyed the *Asuras* (Demons). Finally, all their prayers were accepted. A daughter was born in their house. *Rajguru* saw her horoscope and said, "O Queen" you are very lucky, all the subjects of this daughter of yours will become followers, she will become their guide. It will remove the darkness of ignorance from their lives. The parents affectionately named herGoutami and Maha Prajapati in the government governance list, a few years later the couple was blessed with another daughter. Extremely beautiful just like the goddess of Mayalok, There was no labour maid to the queen at the time of her birth as if someone had magically sent this girl to the earth. The parents seeing her appearance, nature and the awe-inspiring atmosphere around her, named her - Mahamaya. According to tradition, the elder sister is married first. The king of the republic expanded his kingdom by marrying the princesses of other republics. Shuddhodhan's father sent a special request to Kapilavastu to make Goutami his daughter-in-law. Suddhodhana was a very courageous and mighty prince. After he got married, he had to take charge of his rule and get the title of king. On an auspicious occasion, Suddhodhan was married to Goutami. Goutami had moved to Devdutt from Kapilavastu. She had a special love and affection for her younger sister Mahamaya. She always wondered "how good it would have been if my friendly and simple sister would have been close to me."

It is the law of nature that the kind of emotions or thinking we have,the same kind of situations come before us. As time passed by, Suddhodhana became a skilled and popular ruler, but one of the worries that he always suffered was that he has not yet been able to give a successor to his dynasty. Queen Goutami was extremely worried, that even after going through numerous medical examinations and regularly keeping a track of all the ovulating days after the menstruation cycle, she was also her husband's hope, even the *Rajvaidya (Royal Doctor)* said that *Rani Maa* is completely healthy but still she was unable to bear the child in her womb. After discussing with the educators she sent a marriage proposal for her younger sister Maya to her parents. Mother Pramila also thought that if the girl of another dynasty was brought as daughter-in-law by her tribe, then injustice would be done to Goutami. The queen immediately accepted the offer. Maya came to Kapilavastu as the second wife to Suddhodhana. Goutami had always wished for her sister's companionship, but not in this form. The cycle of circumstances and times changed! Maya was now her husband's wife. Goutami had gladly accepted it, without keeping any hatred or jealousy in her mind. After Maya reached Kapilvastu, things started to change. Maya was sleeping at night in her chamber when she had a wonderful dream of a white elephant approaching her. Which is considered to be a very auspicious sign, in marine science, a white elephant symbolizes pregnancy. Maya then sees in the dream that the nymphs are welcoming her with a lotus in her hand. Maya conceives. According to tradition, a woman's first child is born in her parent's place. Mahamaya was all set to go to her father's house. Goutami also gladly accompanied her younger sister, along with several slave maids, in the palanquin tokapilavastu.When Mahamaya saw the lotus flower in her dream, she knew that the time for her delivery had come. On the way, everyone reached a small village named Lumbini. While there, in the forest of Mallikas, mother Mahamaya gave birth to a child. No one had ever seen a child with such a beautiful and fascinating face. The future king of Kapilvastu has taken birth on earth. As the only goal of Mahamaya's life was this, she had come to this earth only to give birth to a child. Mahamaya's face brightened up with superior arrogance under the full moon rays.Goutami along with her maids got involved in the care of the pregnant mother and very soon Mahamaya left this earth forever and ever by handing over her milk-faced child to her sister. Goutami was till now only a girl and then a married woman. She became a full-fledged mother as she held the gleaming baby in her hands. The cold blood flowing in her body got circulated, the breasts began to stretch, to satisfy the hungry baby, milk automatically filled the breasts. That baby of Mahamaya has now completely become Goutami's. The child Gautam became restless and grew up in the lap of Mother Goutami. When Goutami came back to Kapilvastu, she named the prince with a grand ceremony.The astrologer predicted, "This child will rule the whole earth, or else he will become the mightiest ruler, otherwise a great monk who shows the path to the society, he will excel in the path that he adopts, and prosper in it."

Gautam was given the name "Siddhartha". The king and Goutami made great efforts to keep the child tied in the comforts of the palace so that his mind would not be disturbed by seeing the troubles, miseries and sorrows of the outside world. Goutami brought up the child with a lot of affection and attachment. As a result, the dormant eggs started breathing in her body. The process of progeny in the uterus started becoming very active and mother Goutami gave birth to a very beautiful boy and girl. The girl's name was Sundari and the boy's name is Sundaranand.Nand was a bit different from his elder brother Siddhartha by nature. He was not as calm as his brother. Despite being playful, he had great respect for his elder brother. Siddhartha is now entering the youthful stage, Goutami taught him all the arts that a *Kshatriya* prince should learn. Gave him the world's best horse, Kandak. The wisest charioteer "Channa" was engaged in the service of Gautam and sent Gautam to be victorious in Yashodhara's *swayamvara* so that he could find his desired bride and she becomes a humble, intelligent advisor to the proficient ruler.

King Shuddhodhana used to conduct all the affairs of the state together. She took special care of prince Gautam of the Shakya dynasty. Everyone used to call Siddhartha by the name Gautam, but she could not stop the king's son

Siddhartha from abandoning him. After Yashodhara became pregnant, she was very sure that now Siddhartha would become a skilled ruler. Yashodhara became pregnant after five years of marriage and during these five years, Goutami always lived near Yoshdhara like a shadow. She used to think and guide her regarding ways to attract her husband, her most fertile days and consultation with *Rajvaidyas* (Royal Doctors) because Goutami used to miss her younger sister Mahamaya and she felt that she was a special girl. She used to feel that she was born to fulfil a purpose. And her death after the birth of Siddhartha proved that she had incarnated only to give birth to a great man. She brought up Siddhartha very dearly.She knew how disturbed the person living like a prince is from inside, his mind does not feel in this world of deceit. He is busy in search of truth. But when Yashodhara conceived, she became a little relaxed. A man gets infatuated with a woman and takes courage to conquer that infatuation but a child's endearment is much deeper. This endearment is so tempting that a man's greed, intelligence and even his breath is all tied up with the child. The bond with a child is the strongest. He thought that Siddhartha would never be dissuaded from this infatuation, but it did not happen either. Ruthless Siddhartha left in the darkness of night to become a seeker. Goutami's mind cried fromwithin and she was sceptical, how will she face Yashodhara? How will she console her? How will she add to the broken morale of her husband in this time of trouble, Goutami will now have to take responsibility for every task. For a few years, Goutami spent the next few years in the hope of her missing son returning. Slowly she started getting news of her son's whereabouts, wandering in the forest. He has also learned to meditate he was abandoned by his disciples and lastly he was blessed with *Boudhi Gyan* under the banyan tree. No, he is no more Siddhartha, but rather *'Bhagwan Buddha'* for mankind.

After attaining the *Bodhisattva*, he goes to cities and republics like Kaushambi, Shravasti, Sarnath, Vaishali, Magadha, etc. to preach. Many followers also call him "Gautam Buddha". Goutami's heart fills with affection. Somewhere she is still attached to "Buddha". She can not survive without him. Her husband's kinmanship friend Amritonandan's son Ananda wished to meet Buddha. Goutami herself had seen, how Ananda, being the elder brother of Gautama, loved him so much. He always used to impose his authority on Siddhartha. He used to persuade him to agree to whatever he asked for. Both Ananda and Goutami are waiting for their beloved, after a gap of nine years it is reported that Buddha is visiting Kapilvastu with his monks. Goutami decided in her mind that here on the southern border of the state, she would build a monastery for her so that her prodigal son would be in front of her eyes. While Buddha was giving his discourses in Anupiya town before coming to Kapilvastu, Bhaddiya, Bhrigu, Kimbil, Anuruddha and Devadatta decided to become monks. Anand already wanted to accompany his dear younger brother, but his mother had taken a promise from him that under any circumstances he would not choose Buddha. Physically, Ananda used to reside in the palace, but his mind used to roam around with Shakyamuni. That is why everyone used to call him *"Silent Muni (Monk)"* sometimes as *"Vedic Muni"*, but in the end, Ananda won over the mind of his mother with his reasoning power and became Buddha's disciple. Just like his name Ananda's gentleness in his body was unique. By nature, he was very soft-hearted, had a sharp intellect and intense memory. Goutami saw that the Buddha himself had taken Rahul with him to make him a monk, in this sorrow, the mournful Shuddhodana died in separation.

His daughter-in-law was living a life of a nun even while living in the palace, then Goutami also decided that she too would become a nun. In Buddhism, women could not enter the *Sangha*. However, when the *Kshatriya* prince became a monk, he was accompanied by his barber. The barber also hung all his clothes and ornaments on a tree outside the village and asked the villagers to take whatever they needed. That is how he had gone to the Buddha's refuge with the *Kshatriya* princes, then Ananda requested that "O Bhante, first of all, you should ignite him so that no one in the *varna* system says that the *Kshatriyas* have established their dominance and they are the only ones who deserve the return.

The Buddha also heeded this request of Ananda and was the first to convert him. Sthavira Ananda became the most beloved disciple of Buddha. He always stayed with him. They became his body servants. He had the privilege of becoming the first "Upasthak". It was the biggest act of his life. He had heard most of the discourses. He used to memorize sixty thousand lines at a time. There is still a ray of hope in Goutami's mind. She decided that she would meet Buddha and seek permission to take refuge in the Sangha.All the princesses started requesting Goutami to take permission from her son and give them the privilege of becoming a nun. Goutami decided, a declaration was made in the state, "Whoever wants to become a nun, housewives, unmarried or married women, they should leave their home and go to Vaishali city with me. The journey will be difficult but the result will be supernatural." Hearing Goutami's call, more than five hundred women became eager to accompany her. Family members, brothers and relatives tried tirelessly to stop them.The *Brahmin* community, the *Vaishya* community, the *Kshatriya* brides and the *Shudra* girls all united and appeared in front of the palace of Goutami. Their family members adopted all kinds of policies*"Saam-Daam-Dand-Bheda"* but failed. On the *Ekadashi* of *Chait* month, everyone left Kapilvastu with Goutami Mata forever. All the housewives never got out of their houses. They had not even experienced how difficult a road journey is. Sometimes they found it very tempting to walk on the paved highway, but as soon as the border of the state was over, it used to be difficult to cross the forest and jungles, sometimes to cook the food they did not even get root vegetables, greens and vegetables and at times dry wood was not available light fire, women were following Goutami as her follower. Goutami had now become *Maha Prajapati*. She started managing the whole system. She asked them to follow the Eightfold Path of *Vidhisattva* so that no one has any kind of attachment or illusion and no hope of any kind of happiness and splendour. Following the middle path suggested by the Buddha, after a gap of nine months and a long arduous journey, Goutami with all the followers reached outside the city of Vaishali. She did not enter the splendid Vaishali city, but started living under the open sky in a forest outside the limits of that city and sent the news to meet Buddha, but Gautam Buddha politely declined the offer to meet her. Goutami started thinking that through whom she should convey her words to Bhante. As it is, all the sons of his dear disciples are much respected. Everyone calls him *"Dharma Senapati"*. They talk appropriately and they are knowledgeable of religion, but will they be able to explain to Buddha? Then she got reminded of her *"Vaideh Muni"* Ananda. Soon she reached Anand in his monastery. Ananda, having received news of the arrival of *MahaPrajapati* and her followers, explains to them that only monks are allowed here in the Sangha. Entry of women is prohibited, but Goutami said steadfastly and submissively, "Just as you want to be with your *Guru* forever, seek his company, preach his discourses, serve him, in the same way, I cannot live without Buddha. My last wish is that I should attain Nirvana in front of *Bhante*. I have come with my friends, leaving everything behind including home, family and bondage. We are not all ordained but are leading a life like nuns. The earth is still under my feet, the season is my cover, there is no craving in the mind, I am alive only to be with my Buddha."

Anand's mind was disturbed after hearing such a compassionate request from Goutami, he has been serving Bhante for years now, but hasn't been able to get *Boudhi Gyan* because somewhere in his mind worldly feelings are still alive. He is proficient in argumentative knowledge and he also believes in equality for women. If men can be monks, why can't women? He once asked this question to *Bhante* too. Then Buddha said, I see man and woman equally, but both are gender-different. *Purusha's* consciousness (discretion) is extroverted, he is lustful, he also uses force to get beautiful things. That's why if he finds a woman, he also rapes her. But the woman's consciousness (conscience) is introverted, she believes in giving love.Her dedication intensifies and leads to foolish acts. Both are of different gender. Their consciousness also works in the opposite direction. That is why it is not appropriate for these two to stay together in the Sangh. "Now Anand knows that Bhante can be convinced only through logic. Goutami's renunciation will be the victory of penance. Not everyone can become a bhikshuni, but Goutami is the best, most qualified and authoritative. What is patience? - This Goutami has learned from her daughter-in-law Yashodhara. With the same patience, she waited for her companions, taking food at a time, wearing yellow clothes and shaving their heads. She conveyed her message to *Sakya Muni* through Anand. Anand requested the Lord three times, but the Lord refused his request three times and then Anand thought of persuading the Lord in another way. He asked the Lord, *"Bhante*, can women who are homeless and migrated from home have the vision of *Senapati Phal, Sakrtagami Phal, Anagami Phal,* and *Aharvaka?"* The Lord replied, "Yes, of course, she can enjoy." *Bhante* can she realize? Lord. Well, if women also got the promise to become evangelized, Lord Buddha had to agree to this argument, but he followed eight hard rules for the *bhikshunisangha.* He laid a condition to follow. He placed a provision of eight hard rules for the nuns before Ananda and said that they would have to follow these rules throughout their life. Even if the nuns had attained the sub-estate for a hundred years, they would still be the same as the monks. Will respect them, will respect them as their senior. Under no circumstances will they abuse the monk, never disrespect him, never trespass throughout his life in the observance of the *dharma vinaya* (rule). Buddha's human knowledge (physical, mental, emotional and conscious) is amazing. In this Vinaya system, he reposed more faith in the women, he has also accepted the sexual weakness of the men. They know that being a man (*Purusha-chit*), he is arrogant by nature. Outside the city of Vaishali, all the women with swollen feet, tired and sad are engrossed in meditation. Goutami is sure that, the clever Ananda will surely convince the Buddha. There is a question of penance for their whole life and then it is not only a question of a woman but a question of the existence of the entire female race. Lord Buddha will have to approve, no matter how strict those rules are, they will follow all the rules. Goutami has an extraordinary talent to conduct. She has seen the various seasons of life. Now she wants to spend the rest of the time promoting the policies of Lord Buddha. She does not want to be away from the company of the *Bodhisattva* even for a moment. The evening is slowly setting. The city of Vaishali is lit up with lamps. The women sitting in the border forest look at the darkening sky. They all want liberation from the cycle of life and death, want salvation. Goutami spotted Ananda who was seen coming from afar. It was from the soft smile on Ananda's face that Goutami realized that her penance was successful. Ananda bowed to Maha Prajapati and said, "Your request has been accepted by Bhante." A wave of joy started flowing all around, everyone's sad eyes started shining brighter than those burning oil lamps. Everyone forgot their hunger, fatigue, sadness and silence. Waves of new energy started swaying in their body. Goutami's mind became very happy, but Goutami's journey is not over yet. They have finally gotten permission to join the *Sangh*. In reality, the next stop will be even more difficult for Goutami. The nuns have to follow those hard eight rules. *Sangh* has to be established; it has to be run smoothly.

But eight hard rules have to be followed. The status of a nun will remain one level below that of a monk, however senior she may be in age. She has to pay respect to a monk who is younger than her and never use abusive behaviour. Even if the monk makes a mistake, she will not say anything in front of him and will not make any objection. When Goutami put all the rules one by one in front of the *Sakya* women, they also happily accepted them. Among them were all castes and all classes of marriages, girls, old age, many women had been so exploited in their lives by their husbands that they only wanted liberation.

Someone was abandoned by her husband for the sake of another woman because her husband's heart was now filled with her. Somewhere the girl child used to become a victim of the sexuality of the rich people of the society even before reaching puberty, somewhere the woman was just like an indulgence. They had no identity of their own, she was constantly being a victim of so many socio-economic or sexual tortures, they wanted salvation. They felt that attaining salvation was better than repeatedly taking birth and going through the pain of various difficulties, he did not see any fault in his rules, whereas the bhikshuni sangha was given a slightly lower status in his desire for eternal liberation from suffering from repeated births. It was like a mole compared to the tortures he had experienced in his past. She wanted to live everything just once with her freedom, open her mind, wanted to be converted. Everyone took refuge in the bhikshuni Sangha along with Goutami. Now their greed, vice, delusion, ignorance, craving, and belief in the soul have all vanished forever because the path of Buddha is not the path of knowledge, but the path of will. He is not the first or the last Buddha of this earth, says "Tathagata". Buddha will be born only from Manushi, whose mind is always in *samadhi,* that is wisdom. He never differentiated between man and woman, he saw them as equals but found them different based on the basis of their sexuality. And out of ignorance, he took that ego to be his self-respect.

Throughout his life, he tries his best to keep that self-respecting ego alive. When a woman touches his feet and gives him a high position of deity, then to maintain his self-respect, he starts making his determination and tries to control himself. Men generally look at women with lust. First of all, there is a possibility of the fall in lust in men and women only in men. That is why there is an urgent need to have some tough rules in the Sangh. Misguided monks will be expelled by the Bhikshu Sangh itself, there is no provision for any pardon for them. Many years later, when the Buddha had immigrated to the Nyagodha forest located in Kapilavastu, Goutamifor the first time had proposed to become a bhikshuni. For the second time, Mata Goutami went there again in the *Kutagarshala* of *Mahavan* of Vaishali city and proposed but that too was rejected. Now she had come to the city of Vaishali on foot along with thousands of Shakya women, their swollen injured legs, dusty bodies, their dissected hair, their hair severed head, after looking at such pathetic conditions Ananda could not stop himself. When she stood outside the bracket door of the cottage for the third time, Ananda had to plead with Bhante by taking her side, but when Bhante politely refused for the third time, Anand reasoned, "Oh Bhante, you ask my question. Answer: Can women attain *Sotapati* fruit, *Sakridagami* fruit, *Anagami*fruit, and *Aharva* in the *Praveed* religion? Bhante replied, "Yes Ananda", then Ananda asked, "If the women who were admitted to the religion professed by *Bhante* Tathagata can appear to Aharva, then the guardian, Kshirdayika, Poshika, your aunt, who gave you her milk, should get *Pravajya*". Bhante gave his approval, but he put some difficult rules in entering the bhikshuni Sangha, which is called *"Ashtaguru Dhamma"*.

Goutami starts waiting for the sunrise. Tomorrow is the start of a new chapter. The *Sangh* was established and Goutami had the privilege of becoming the first female nun. Lord Buddha himself ordained her and made her the directress of the *Sangh*.

❑

Yashodhara

King Suppabuddha of the *Koliya*dynasty was very happy today. Today a beautiful girl has been born to him. He has great affection for his first son Devdutt but always prayed to his presiding deity for a daughter and when the maid came and gave the good news that Queen Pamita had given birth to a beautiful girl, he has since then become overjoyed. He wants to get up quickly and reach the inner palace, but after the delivery, he will not be able to go to his wife and the newborn baby for forty days. Worshipping and praying have been stopped in the royal family because of Sutak. Playful Devdutt is also very happy that he now has a younger sister on whom he can run his orders. The forty days of Sutak ended on the Trayodashi moon of Chaitra month. The maid came and gave a message, "Your Majesty, get ready for today's naming ceremony. *Raj Purohit* (royal priest) will come and name this *Kshatrani* princess. Your daughter is as beautiful as a goddess." After hearing this the king's mind became eager to see his daughter. Soon after taking a bath, he went to the shrine. There Queen Pamita is already sitting on a wooden track with her daughter wrapped in silk cloth in her lap on a wooden plank. There is still time to light the fire in *Havanakund*. *Raj Jyotish* came with great humilityandgreeted the king and queen. The method of worship started with the chanting of *mantras*. The whole atmosphere was filled with devotion. The king would occasionally look at the girl wrapped in clothes and repeat the *mantra* with the priest. Prince Devdutt is not interested in all these activities. He went to play with horses with the son of the commander. At the end of the puja, the pandit said, "Your Majesty, you bless your daughter and name it. This is the auspicious time."

King Suppabuddha took his daughter in his arms, as soon as he removed the silk cloth, he saw that the face of a soft white girl like a cotton ball, "my mother" came out of his mouth. The child's face and smile resembled his mother's. For a moment it felt like "Mother" herself had come to his house after taking re-birth. His mother was a wise woman. She used to understand the secrets of everyone's mind in a blink of an eye and would also tell the solution to every problem. Looking lovingly at the queen, he said - "Gopa" this is our Gopa mother. We will call her Gopa. The queen happily nodded her head in agreement. *Raj Jyotish* while calculating the planets said - "Your majesty, this girl has been born in the combination of very rare constellations. She will always be remembered in all three worlds. This girl is a miraculous combination of glory and patience, now I will do her royal naming ceremony. From today onwards, she will be an idol of glory and patience for the whole earth and will be known by the name of "Yashodhara". The king and queen are very happy with the prediction of their daughter. The naming ceremony of the king's beloved 'Gopa' was successful.

Gopa is now 14 years old. Only a few months have passed since she menstruated. According to tradition, her marriage has to be announced. Now she is a very beautiful adolescent girl. Puberty is just now knocking, but youth is nowhere to be seen. Gopa is extremely calm and discreet. All her friends tell the secret stories of their minds to her only. *Rajguru*has taught her all kinds of scriptures. *Kshatriniyas* could read *Vedas* and *Puranas*. That's why she got educated in it. Father consult *Rajguru* as to where to marry her. A suitable girl needs only a suitable groom, which is a difficult problem. Like an ordinary father, the king's mind is also anxious. *Rajguru* advised - "O your majesty, let's conduct a *swayamvara*. Get the princess married to the best *Aryaputra*. The announcement of *swayamvara* resonated from the Himalayas to the banks of the Ganges. The kings of all the states wanted the daughter of the Koliya dynasty to become their daughter-in-law so that they could expand their kingdoms. The marriage ceremony among the *Kshatriyas* is a worthy occasion to showcase their potential. The prince of the *Shakya* dynasty also attended the *swayamvar*. Quite eyes with very charming sight, stoutly beautiful body with a sweet smile when she entered the *swayamvar*, that very moment Gopa prayed and asked him from her deity. Competition is very difficult but in front of the orders of the creator, all the helpless, very strong, clever, audaciously angry NandarjunaNagdatta was defeated by the *Shakya* dynasty prince. No one could understand this. All the people jumped with joy, Gopa, choosing the prince, bowed down to the deity in her heart.

There is a lot of hustle and bustle in Kapilvastu. *Maha Prajapati* Goutami jumped in joy. The younger brother is amazed and rejoiced at the victory of his elder brother. Shuddhodana has completely opened the royal treasury. Donations are being given to the poor. The whole city is decorated like newlyweds. In childhood, seeing a swan being shot with an arrow, the child who had cried with sorrow and who was always lost in contemplation, who never used weapons, the same young prince is today returning to his kingdom after his victory along with the very beautiful, patient, intelligent *Kshatrani* Yashodhara. Blessed is Prince Siddhartha, now he can be sure that he will take *sannyas* by handing over his royal palace to the prince and daughter-in-law. That is why breaking the limitless limits of happiness, we are donating all the money deposited in our treasury. "Gopa" became Yashodhara after coming to her in-laws' house. Father's beloved Duhita has become a duty-worthy daughter-in-law here. All the slaves and the women of the family have a special affection for her. Such is her nature. Whoever talks to her once, becomes her own forever. Queen Goutami gave all the diamond and ruby studded jewellery of her treasure to Yashodhara. Whenever she used to wear those ornaments, she glowed like the goddess of the temple, no one could take their eyes off her even if they wanted to. The experienced Goutami knows about the nature of her son. It has been ordered that every day Yashodhara's makeup should be done in different forms. Her room should always be filled with aromatic fragrances. The maids are also smart and understand everything. They continue to teach Yashodhara the lessons of wooing her husband. Naive Yashodhara also follows everyone's advice. Now Yashodhara and Siddharth are famous as the most beautiful, prestigious and sensible married couple in this world. When both of them walked in their garden together, it seemed as if they complemented each other. All the parents of the state started longing to get the pair of their future children in this form. When Siddhartha was in deep contemplation, Yashodhara never hindered his devotion or yoga, just silently followed him. Whenever Yashodhara served him food with love, the prince would get hurt in his heart, "Ah this bond". Five years have passed just like this. Mother Goutami explained to her daughter-in-law "When a woman gives birth to a child, only then she is complete." Now you too will have to produce children for your descendants. Siddhartha should also feel his duty". In due course of time, Yashodhara conceived. This news also spread to everyone within ten days. Now when pregnant Yashodhara went in front of her husband, Siddhartha kept staring at her. But the hidden expression behind that sight, the secrecy would have been read by Gopa hurriedly - "Ah: one more bond" and becomes sad. Kusla Dai would take full care of her but no one could understand the pain in her mind. Days slowly passed by. Now Yashodhara lives with her maidservants and mother Goutami in the inner maternity room of the inner palace. It is not possible to even meet the husband. On the other hand, Tathagata has also become impatient. The temptation to see their children can become a hindrance to their ascetic life. He will not be able to break the attachment of a father towards his son. They have to decide soon. Yashodhara gave birth to a son after enduring immense pain and labour pain for two nights. This news was much more joyful than the news of Siddhartha's birth, mother Goutami and father Suddhodhana were overjoyed at the arrival of their grandson. They have to do a lot to welcome him, they started preparing for the same.

The first half of the night, Kusla Dai is still resting and the mother is sleeping with her newborn son in the room outside the maternity room. There is a strange silence in the entire room. The wheel of time began and slowly Siddhartha entered that room. There was stability in the particles of nature as if for a few moments the earth stopped rotating on its axis. Those moments of time stopped a while. No human being from the three worlds came to know what the law of nature is creating. The twelfth-day moon of *Krishna Paksha's Dwadashi* became even slower. Siddhartha quietly left the room and started walking out of his palace, to the border of his kingdom. Reaching outside the state border, he saw the shining pole star in the deep black sky spreading above and made his steps towards the east. During the four hours of that night, the birds stayed in their nests, the animals did not move on the way. The rivers flowed in silence; there was no noise of any kind. It was early in the morning that Siddhartha sacrificed everything and left, but in the second half of the night, nature also remained silent about what conversation happened between Yashodhara and Siddhartha in that room. Water, air, the fire of the lamp, sky, earth, none was a witness to the event. Tathagata had come out with permission from Yashodhara or there was a lot of argument between them. Yashodhara herself had allowed him to go as an idol of renunciation or tried to stop him by praying persuasion. She may also have been very angry because Siddhartha had won her in the swayamvara and brought her as his wife. If a family life was not to be followed, then why should the husband and wife have physical relations? Why did you wish to have children? Or it may also happen that there has been no communication between them, hemight have lost the courage to face his wife, after seeing the face of the newborn baby, he might get tied in the infatuation of his son, thinking that leaving his wife and son sleeping outside the door of the room, he set out on his own in search of truth. Secretly, silently, he became great in his search for truth and left behind Yashodhara completely alone with her newborn baby. The married women of the city would either show sympathy or taunt them, "What is the life of such a woman? Despite so much beauty and opulence, she could not keep a man tied up. How weak and unsuccessful a housewife she is." *Hat Bhagini Si Yashodhara* lived quietly, patiently accepting all the accusations, slanders, reproaches, taunts, insults and pity. The midwife explained - "Your son is breastfeeding, eat sufficient nutritious food, do not keep any worries in your mind, otherwise it will affect the child". So MatruopaYashodhara, like a compassionate woman, engaged in the upbringing of her son, according to the custom, on the fortieth day after the *royal yajna*, his naming ceremony was held and he was named Rahul, meaning efficient, conqueror of sorrow, capable. When *Rajguru* gave this name, Yashodhara pulled him towards her chest, but everyone knew that no skilled able conqueror can end Yashodhara's sorrows. Suddhodhanawas unable to see his daughter-in-law in her eyes. SeriousGoutami was only making an impression of her presence felt. In the feeling of extreme sadness Siddhartha's only son who was born from the womb of Yashodhara, the *Kshatriya* prince's naming ceremony was completed.

No one can stop the speed of time. The intelligent, playful Rahul is now growing up. He always questions his mother regarding his father "Father has gone in search of truth. He is a great man, has become a hermit for the betterment of sacrament." Yashodhara answers him saying something like this, now he does not even drink mother's milk. For the prince, all kinds of nutritious food have been arranged in the palace. Since the time Rahul quit drinking his mother's milk and started taking other diet, the blood flowing in mother's arteries has started cooling. Now it does not flow completely pure from the heart. Iron stored in blood also dries up like breast milk. Her breathing process is slow enough to just keep her alive. Now the coolness of the moonlight, the warmth of sunlight, the fast flow of rivers and the waves, nothing can move her body. Her mind has become samadhi. She has become noetic. Those who are doing penance and yoga in Tathagat's Forest, away from their family and society, Yoshodhra is destroying her craving in the same penance. Now she is neither angry about the departure of her husband nor is she waiting for his return. What was once said by everyone to be an obstacle on the path of her husband's accomplishment, she has now attained "*Siddhi*". The deep pain of separation also can not harm her now. Rahul has a resemblance to his father and the absence of his father is filed by his grandfather. Maharaj Shuddhodhana rekindles the golden dream of the future of his kingdom in his only descendant. He considers himself guilty of his daughter-in-law. That is why he continues to dedicate everything to his grandson Rahul with a lot of affection, love and caress.

Nature took a turn yet again. The *Nagpasha* time came around yet again. The *Rajguru* came to *Maharaja* Shuddhodhana and said, "Buddha himself is coming to the city. He will come here with his monks. Talk to his followers. Blessings will be given. It is our good fortune that Lord Buddha will visit us." The fatherly emotion of the king rose again, he immediately ordered - "The whole state should be decorated with flowers to welcome Lord Buddha. The townspeople should bow down on both sides of the highway, welcome them and worship them. Their stay should be arranged in *Raj Prasad*". But *Maharaj*, he is no longer our beloved Siddhartha. Now he has become a 'complete noetic' Buddha. Lord Buddha will not live in the palace with the monks. Separate arrangements have to be made for them. As if Maharaj's dream was broken in between. Ruthless game of destiny, the son is coming back but has become Buddha, has become God. Now no social or family relationship can be attached to him. A sharp pain arose in his heart, yet his mind is happy. The human mind is very greedy. There is always hope of getting something or the other. Even before going to the face of death, he wants to live a few more moments. Sudhodhana is also no exception. Goutami's mind has also become very excited but she is worried about her daughter-in-law. That daughter-in-law now does not even remember her previous birth, how she had to bear the separation of her husband in her previous life as well. How arrogant was the princess back then. *Bodhisattva* was blessed by the Malang elephant and chosen from among the thousands of people present on the highway, but only after marriage, when the queen's mother told her that this son belonged to the same king, how she had to flee into the jungles to protect her life during pregnancy. She gave birth to that child in the forest, he was brought up there but in the cycle of time, he was chosen for the daughter of the king of the same kingdom. The queen had told the truth to the princess. Her son was given strict orders to be a hermit so that he could not get married to his own sister. The princess had cried a lot and had gone to the astrologer for solutions. Astrologer had said, "He will not be able to be your husband in this birth. Yes, you will be born again and you will certainly be able to become the mother of a *Bodhisattva's* child." The princess gave up her life in her virginity, her husband became a hermit and attained salvation. Now in this life, she could not become the wife of Buddha, but she got the good fortune of becoming Rahul's mother. Now she does not remember anything from her past life. She too has become a hermit. She takes food only once a day, has renounced her clothes, sacrificed her silk clothes and has wrapped herself in a colourless cotton cloth. She did not comb her hair and did not take care of her fragile body. The jewellery has been returned to Mother Goutami. Worldly pleasures and indulgences have been completely abandoned. She was waiting patiently to qualify. She has heard stories of Lord Buddha from the maidservants, how a wealthy merchant of a city had immense wealth. With how pompously he had welcomed Buddha. The monks had brought so many fruits, flowers, food and chives as a gift to the *Sangh*, but when the hungry, weak, helpless, supremely devout old mother offered only a mango to the Lord, the Lord himself accepted that alms. All the monks looked at Buddha in amazement. The rich merchant hesitantly asked, "O Lord, I have presented you with food with such reverence, but why did you only accept a ripe small mango from that old lady? Is there something lacking in my hospitality or devotion?" Then Buddha humbly replied - "O worshiper. You have given me some part of your immense wealth, but this old mother has nothing, she has not even eaten a grain for many days, yet she has given her all that she had i.e., a mango, which she has donated to me in alms. Now tell me, how can I refuse the alms of the worshiper who gives everything she has? The rich merchant spoke up -"*Bhante* you are great and merciful. Bless us". Only the one who donates his dearest thing to Buddha receives his blessings. Yashodhara has heard so many stories, teachings and discourses through her maidservants and now the Arhat himself is returning to his kingdom. To beg from his mother and his wife.

As soon as Lord Buddha entered the city, people gathered around him like an ocean. His beloved '*Kantak*', who was tied in the stables, also got the smell of his master's arrival and was eager to meet him. Its level best to break the bondage tied around its neck. Siddhartha's favourite charioteer Channa was also eager to see his Shakya Muni. It was the same charioteer with whom Prince Siddhartha used to visit the city and inquire about the events and scenes around him. With a lot of compassion, he used to look at the old man standing on the road. How sad was his heart seeing the condition of the sick, helpless old man? Always living in the splendour of the palace, when the prince rode on a chariot went to the city, Shuddhodhana Maharaj would have ordered the residents of the city in advance to keep the city beautifully decorated. Siddhartha should only see the people engrossed in the splendour of happiness all around. No painful sight or sensitive incident should happen in his path. Charioteer Channa always took him towards the east or north direction and tried lifelessly that no sad thoughts or sad incidents should happen during his visit, but destiny plays its game. He had not seen the children playing with joy, youth merging in merriment, deep indifference on the faces of citizens immersed in poverty sloping waist, weak eyesight and old men walking with the support of wooden sticks with their trembling hands and finally in 'the funeral procession'. Seeing all this, his mind was disturbed, "What is the reason for their sorrows?" This question bothered him time and again. There used to be a time when charioteer 'Channa' used to solve all his doubts, today he wants to touch the feet of *Bhante*. Buddha has an answer to every question. Only he will sail my boat across this elusive world. By saying this in the ears of *Kathak,* he also freed the horses so that they too can get freedom from this cycle of life. King Shuddhodana and Mother Goutami themselves walked on the highway to welcome *"Shakya Muni"*. All the townspeople were as if caught in some hypnotic force. This form of *Bhante* had completely hypnotized them. The *"Sakya Muni"*along with his beloved disciple Ananda and the monks chanting mantra, the whole earth had become like *"Buddhmay"*. There was no pain, no anguish, no jealousy, and no competition. All were unifying with Buddha. Monks do not have to stay in Kapilvastu for a long time. After taking alms from his mother and sister-in-law, Tathagat once again proceeded to JaitavanVihar. This is the most important stage of his path to Nirvana. After becoming a *sannyasin*, a monk has to go to his family once with an alms pot. Suddhodana was blessed to see his son in this form. The eyes of *MahaprajapatiGoutami* welled out of love. Younger brother Nand is also astonished to see this form of his brother. He is from Gautam's friend's family but he has great respect and affection for his elder brother. He got married just a few days ago. After seeing his elder brother, he immediately returned to his palace with his newly wedded wife because without her he could not live even for a moment. Yashodhara's friends have also come to the *Nari Mahal* today. All of them want to see *"Shakya Muni"* together. The maidservants are narrating the full description of every moment to Yashodhara. They are requesting "Go and pay respect to your husband Buddha, see him, seek his blessings". But Yashodharawas not restless. She did not even show any impatience to see him. Along with her son, she patiently waited for Lord Buddha to arrive at the palace. She saw Tathagat along with his monks walking on the highway of the city for alms. All of them are well dressed in their clothes. Yashodhara's eyes lit up upon seeing the grand, serene scene. She looked at the boy Rahul and introduced him by giving *darshan* of his unseen father, as the boy Rahul used to inquire about his father every day, Yashodhara said - "Whose whole body is filled with signs of great men. Whose blood characters are well marked with the chakra symbol - the best, whose *Anjan Varna* is *Sunil*

Kesh. Those who have pure frontal light like *Kanchan Patta*. Who has eyebrows like a rainbow, who has a face like full moon, whose mind is distinguished by modesty and *samadhi*, who has left home for a public interest, who looks like a lion among males, he is your father. Rahul identified his father through the introduction given by his mother. The huge sandalwood bed has been lying deserted for years. Yashodhara has never slept on that bed since Siddhartha's abdication and neither wants to sleep anymore. She has brought up her son with great patience and efficiency, tied in the chain of household life. How easy it is to do penance in monasteries away from family on top of forests, mountains and hills, but how rare, difficult and painful it would have been to become a sannyasin by living in social bonds, living in all the facilities of enjoyment and luxury, discovering the truth of one's life. Only Yashodhara has the experience with this. After meeting the parents, brothers, family and residents of the city, Ananda politely asked - "*Bhante* when will you go to Yashodhara Rani to take alms." Tathagat kept quiet. Ananda keeps the capacity to When Lord Buddha came to know about this, he started walking towards Yashodhara's palace and he said - "I am free but Yashodhara is not free yet. She hasn't seen me for so long. She must be very sad. Even if she touches me, don't stop her. Yashodhara's strength is the reason behind the blessings that I have attained. Her kindness never discouraged me. It is the result of her virtuous grace in my life that I have become a *Samyak Buddha*." The room brightened from all directions. The filthy confinement in the room was transformed into boundless peace. The darkness filled with self-blame disappeared on its own, the whole room lit up with a golden aura. *Sakya Muni* is coming, every corner started indicating the arrival of *Sakya Muni*.

Buddha is standing in front of Yashodhara with his almspot. Their son Rahul elatedly asked, Mother, look who is he? Yashodhara said without looking at him said, "Son, this is your father, bow down". Ever since Rahul opened his eyes, he has been brought up in the company of a hermitess, a saintly mother. He has got all the facilities to enjoy the kingdom. His grandfather Sudhodhan has a great influence on his childhood. He has always seen his grandfather with jewellery studded crown wearing silk clothes sitting on the throne surrounded by warriors, charioteers and *Rajguru* in their pomp costumes. He never knew how a monk looks like nor had he ever seen a monk. His coiled hair was tied up, wearing yellow clothes, without any jewellery on his body, no gold earrings in his long ears, without weapons in his hands, but an almspot, with awe he starts looking into the eye of the handsome, calm, giant human, he gets hypnotized by the first sight of his father. 'Where were you for so many years?' Buddha lovingly ran his hands over Rahul's head and remained silent. Rahul did not get his answer, but he got overwhelmed by the presence of his father as if a child has found his most beloved thing that was lost. He was eager to give this message to his grandfather. With permission from his mother, he went to Sudhodhan to describe the looks of his father. Buddha is still standing in front of Yashodhara with an almspot. Yashodhara raised her eyes to look at *Bhante.* 'Buddha himself is standing in front of Yashodhara. For a few moments, she remembered her *swayamvar*, how Siddhartha defeated Nagdutt, showcased his bravery, garland, *panigrahan*, both going for hunting, on the full moon night how they used to swing under the moonlight, courtship, closeness, love but when she looked at Tathagat then she got to know that he is not Siddhartha. Siddhartha was someone else. He is Buddha, *Sakya Muni*. Thousands of men and women are his followers. He is the path exhibitor to nirvana. Yashodhara spoke politely- "Bhante I am offering you my most beloved thing in alms, please accept it". *Trikaldarshi Bhante* understood her mind. He happily accepted his son Rahul.

Understand every sign of his master. His answers also lie in his silence. He understood that today *Bhante* will not go for alms. After sunset, monks do not go to anyone's door for alms. During the entire night, the goddess of sleep could not enter Yashodhara's eyes even for a moment. Buddha also remained still in a calm posture. Tomorrow's sunrise is going to change history. The monks do not have even the slightest indication of what was going to happen tomorrow. All their friends of Yashodhara have left, they are thinking that how can such an arrogant woman be their friend who is not even going to see her husband after years. They left, leaving their cruel, ruthless mistress alone. Yashodhara just said this to the maids and friends who were leaving, "If I have any qualities, then *Aryaputra* himself will come to me. I will worship him only when he comes."

Rahul is a sound-minded child with a feeling of compassion. He has deep respect and love for his father. He will happily become a follower of his father. As Buddha started to leave after the donation, Yashodhara politely folded her hands and said – "*Bhante* please bless me". If the monk has taken the donation, he will have to bless her. As soon as he raised his hands to bless her that very moment Yashodhara said I am Kshatrani. *Brahmins* are of the opinion that schedule cast and women are not entitled to attain salvation. She cannot get rid of the cycle of birth and death for ages to come. In any religion they are not entitled to salvation *Bhante*, will women never be able to attain salvation? What kind of religion is this that differentiates among the human race, according to their gender they are seen in opposite ways? I have offered you my most beloved thing. You bless me with nirvana, Buddha remained silent. Till now women are prohibited to be a part of this community. Buddha has taught only one thing- the world has sorrows, sorrows have reasons, sorrows have solutions and there are ways to remove the sorrows. Tathagata has imparted to his followers the four noble truths, the Eightfold Path, the Paramita, and the *Panchsheel*teachings. "Bodhi" can be attained only by the fulfilment of all the Paramitas, a complete understanding of the Four Noble Truths and the cessation of karma while walking on the Eightfold Path and only after attaining *"Bodhi"* (knowledge) one can get freedom from the cycle of life and death of the world. Any ordinary person can attain Nirvana by following these paths. By conquering the ten *paramitas*, charity, modesty, selflessness, wisdom, semen, peace, truth, *adhishthana*, friendship and neglect, one moves towards enlightenment. Lord Buddha knows that Yashodhara has moved towards *"Buddhatva"* by keeping an unbiased attitude in the refuge of Buddha, in the refuge of religion, without taking refuge in the Sangh. Now she is no more an abandoned woman of her husband, statue of separation, disgrace, bearer of extreme sorrow Siddhartha's companion. Now she is not even a hindrance to the path of truth, rather she has already attained the truth before coming to the refuge of Buddha. No worldly attachment can bind her. She is beyond the experiences of happiness and sorrow. Beyond that, Buddha is silent. Yashodhara has become a nun by living in a householder's life, living in a royal palace, living in the midst of indulgent luxury and pompous materials. Yashodhara is at the level of *"samyak-sambodhi"* (the most excellent). Buddha leaves after bowing down. Today Yashodhara has protected the honour of all women. She has protected their rights. She has protected their existence. "After the tacit approval of Buddha, this *Shakya Kulvadhu* became a *bhikshuni* with *Mahaprajapati*Goutami. She attained *Parinirvana* at the age of 78, two years before Buddha's *Mahanirvana*.

Siddhartha, Tathagata could not have become Buddha without the sacrifice of that great woman. Even though the story of this woman has not been specially written in golden words in the pages of history, but Yashodhara is alive within every woman in some form or the other.

❑

Sujata

Several thousand years ago, the system of society was decided on the basis of birth, not based on *karma*. The subjects were always mesmerized by the divinity of the king, sometimes they used to be attracted by the invisible and latent king and sometimes they feared him. The people of Aruwela region were basically dependent on agriculture. Along with agriculture, cattle rearing was also their other occupation. Most of the *Yaduvanshi* people used to make their living from cattle rearing. In the same feudal era, a very healthy and beautiful girl was born in the house of a cowherd. After many years of prayers, this child was born to them. They named the girl Sujata. She was the only child of her parents, so she was brought up with a lot of pampering and love. They were not poor, but they did not even come from the rich class, so from childhood itself, Sujata had to take the responsibility for animal husbandry. During the day she used to take the cows for grazing, bathe in the river and roam the whole day with her cows in the valleys. From childhood, she became very adept at the task of rearing cows. There was a lack of humility in nature and decency in her conduct. Growing up in the free environment of nature, she had grown into a beautiful young woman.

In those days, girls used to get married at a young age, but a suitable groom for Sujata had not yet been found.

Once when she was returning to her house in the evening after grazing cows, a wealthy Yaduvanshi named orphan Pindik came to her house for business. At the very first sight, the guest realized how efficient this girl was in her work. He also had a son who was very angry and cruel by nature. No humble or gentle-natured woman would be suitable for him. He was in search of a healthy, efficient and skilful girl to bring the son on the right path and handle his huge business. There is no need for the consent of the poor father's young daughter, so like a cow, Sujata was tied from one house to another with a peg. After marriage, Sujata took over all the work with great skill by staying at her in-laws' house, but her husband always remained aloof from her. The lack of affection, love and belongingness was ingrained in her practical life. Sujata often used to get sad at night, then her dearest maid Poorna would share her happiness and sorrows. It is the nature of a woman that she can tolerate poverty but can never tolerate disobeying her husband. His unsatisfied soul is always disturbed, in the full moon of *Chaitra* month, a *yajna* is organized at their home. Sujata offered prayers at many places and performed *yajna* but was in vain. Neither did she get the love of her husband nor children. When she returned after taking a bath from the river in the night of the full moon of *Chaitra* month, when her husband saw her in wet clothes, a wave of lust ran in him. He hugged Sujata to his chest and took him to his bedroom. Sujata had taken a bath and worshiped under a Ajpala Nigrodha tree on the banks of Niranjana River and had wished for a child from the tree god, O God, give me the good fortune of becoming a mother, fulfil this wish of mine, after having a child, I will come to you every year. I will offer *prasad* and worship. She didn't even feel any fear in that waning moon. After taking a bath alone, she reached her home. The eyes of the husband that always alienated her had now fallen for her, while having sex in the bedroom with her husband in her mind, she started feeling that her prayer had been accepted. For the first few months, she would regularly offer prayers in front of the tree deity after bathing in the river. The seed had come in her womb, now after the seventh month, she stopped going out of her house. Kundalakeshi maid started taking special care of pregnant Sujata. Poorna was not only a maidservant but the only companion of her happiness and sorrow. Now Sujata is no longer sad but is content feeling proud of being a mother.

On the ninth day of nine months, Sujata gave birth to a very beautiful boy. According to tradition, she still cannot go out of the house, she has to stay with her new-born child in the maternity room for forty days. As Sujata started getting a little better, she ordered her caretakers to give the milk of a thousand cows to five hundred cows and then the milk of those five hundred cows to a hundred cows and then the milk of those hundred cows to her dearest eight cows so that they give the most nutritious and condensed milk. Then after making pudding of the same milk, she will offer it to the tree deity. She has special care to offer prayers after the fulfilment of her wish. *Vaishakh Purnima* will be on the fourteenth day, which she has calculated from the *Hindu* calendar. She called out for Poorna, where are you Poorna, clean around the Ajpala Nigrodha tree, it has been a long time, I have not gone for darshan. Taking prasad on the full moon day of *Vaishakh*, I will go to seek blessings along with my son. Poorna immediately moved towards the mound. Going there, what does she see, a dead skeleton body doing penance sitting ascetic. The vines of the tree are wrapped around it, termites, snakes have all surrounded it, but the ascetic is neutral, blinding his eyes in the posture of severe penance. Far away at a port, five more monks are sitting in meditation. Innocent Poorna started trembling after seeing this scene. The broom from her hand and she came back home running. A panting Poorna spoke up, *Devi* Sujata the elusive deity is seated there, the deity of the tree god himself has appeared and is sitting in a yoga posture.

Sujata said, Poorna go and clean the place. By handing over her son to Kundalakeshi, Sujata with great care got busy making Prasad. After the birth of the child, today for the first time she entered the kitchen. Cleaned the whole kitchen with water and then made *kheer* with the milk of her beloved cows by placing a pan on the stove. Sujata, the daughter-in-law of the wealthy Yaduvanshi, took out a golden vessel from her chest, poured *kheer* in it, and started walking with reverence to offer the tree deity with flowers, rice, incense and a lamp on the golden plate. On the other hand, even after forty-nine days of severe penance, Tathagata did not get knowledge, for the last seven years he is wandering. *Sadhaks* also learned the practices of yoga *samadhi* from *Guru Aalar Kalam* and *UddakaRamaputra*, did hard penance without food and water and did not attain *Bodhi Gyan* even after giving endless tortures to his body. This morning some *sakhis* were going to take a bath on the banks of river Niranjana and were singing a very melodious folk song.

O Aali, don't stretch the strings of my *veena* too much, know that oh friend, don't leave the strings of my *veena* too loud, it will not sound melodious, then Aali, know how to play the strings of the veena, don't stretch too much or leave too much, see melodious how it will sound know this.

It was the deep meditating state of Tathagata that was disturbed. This is the essence of life, too much of anything is inappropriate, neither enjoyment nor yoga. He was infused with human qualities, the desire to take human food was awakened. As soon as Tathagata opened his eyes, he found a woman standing in front of him in a devotional posture with humility and a golden pot of porridge (kheer). Sujata looked at the face of the same ascetic, how calm, simple and compassionate that sight is. A supernatural light is shining on the face of the ascetic, his coiled hair, long ears, long neck, everything is so attractive. He is so calm despite his skeletal physique. As if Sujata has received darshan of god, she said, 'Arya's son, the human form, accept my salutation. Accept this *prasad* of mine, may your blessings always be with me. O son of God, accept my service. Tathagata after bathing at the ghat of Niranjana river sat down again under that tree and with great reverence took the pot of porridge to his mouth. While he was having the porridge, Sujata started praying before that ascetic with folded hands with closed eyes, as my wish has been fulfilled, may your wish also be fulfilled. She kept looking at that godly man with love, she internally felt as if she had gotten complete today. Whatever void was there in her life for so many years, has been filled by the mere sight of this yogi. She was filled with a base of humility, compassion, love and faith. Poorna was also surprised to see such a condition of hers. She said, get up, now let's go home, your family is waiting for you. As if Sujata has woken up from a dream, she is a virtuous married woman. As soon as she started leaving after bowing to him, Tathagata said Goddess, your porridge has satisfied my soul, when I attain knowledge, I will surely come to your house and bless your family. Sujata walked towards her home in the form of a complete woman, but the five seekers of Kaudinya etc. of Tathagata got angry. They strongly condemned the process of breaking Tathagata's strict penance and accepting porridge from the hands of a woman and separated from Tathagata. Tathagata left for Gaya alone in search of knowledge and took a farewell from the fighter village. This was the last stage of his extreme penance; he proceeded alone on the path of Nirvana. It was not that in the enlightenment of *Bodhi* he was the only one to have porridge, even *Vipassi* Buddha from Sundasana Seth's daughter, Kakusangha Buddha from Vajirindha, Kassapa Buddha himself took porridge from his wife Sunanda. Gautam has taken porridge from Sujata. Sujata is now back in her house, but even though her mind is complete, she no longer feels homely. She is searching for her being. The girl who has moved independently from childhood wants to return to the lap of nature. She does not like the wealth and opulence of her husband; her mind does not match the harsh nature of her husband. She wants to remain calm like that ascetic, but there is no escape from worldly bondage. She has to be in the family for her little child. Later, she also got the news that the ascetic Gautam has now become Gautam Buddha. He attained Bodhi Gyan only after consuming her porridge, and one night she hugged Poorna and started crying out loud. Oh friend, that ascetic became a Buddha after having my prasad and I am unfortunate till now. I also want freedom from this body, from my soul. Innocent Poorna has no answer and no solution for that. She is only a silent witness to Sujata's heartache.

Just as Tathagata had promised, after some years he along with his disciples and monks, came to fighter village from Sravasti. They reached the house of orphan Pindik for alms. At home, his daughter-in-law was quarrelling with her husband in a very loud tone angrily. The father-in-law got a little ashamed, but there was no humility in the voice of the daughter-in-law, nor did she lower her voice. Buddha calmly sat outside the door. He could not go back without taking alms from the housewife's hand. The daughter-in-law came out and was astonished to see the ascetic himself in front of her and quickly started bowing at his feet. Buddha asked Goddess did you recognize me. Yes, son of God, I have been waiting for you for years. Buddha said I am a monk, not a son of a god. After having the porridge from your hands, I attained enlightenment. I have come to your door for alms. Sujata said, Lord, what can an ordinary woman like me offer you, but all of you will have to accept my hospitality. Let me arrange for food here itself. I request all of you to please accept it. Gautam Buddha said, O Goddess, there is so much discord in your house, food should be cooked and reached with a calm mind and a sense of joy, only then it will be edible. Bewildered Sujata kept looking at Buddha. Buddha said peace at home is always in the hands of a woman, it is the duty of a wife to maintain her married life peacefully with her husband. There are seven types of wives.

Vadhik Sama - Those who are like a butcher, want to harm their husband, want to kill him, are very cruel in nature.

Chor Sama - Such wives are very greedy, they take pleasure in spending the money of the husband and they do not save.

Pramad Sama - She is very lazy in nature, never helps in household chores. She is always busy gathering her means of entertainment.

Bhagni Sama - Who loves her husband like a sister, remains intimately attached to him and always prays for his good wishes.

Sakhi Sama - The one who keeps a friendly relationship with her husband, keeps a sense of friendship, always supports him in every happiness and sorrow.

DaasiSama - Who treats her husband as her master and has a sense of service, does not cause any kind of trouble but serves him uninterruptedly in all his troubles.

Sujata listens to all the words silently with tearful eyes and says to the Lord, I don't know which of these seven categories I belong to. I am a married woman full of human qualities. In my married life, when I see the unfulfilled desires of my heart, I behave raucously. Sorry, it won't happen now. Buddha blessed her and went back. After that, Sujata followed her wife's *dharma* with utmost devotion, but her troubled mind sometimes asked that if there are seven types of wives, then how many types are there of husbands? Does he remain of one type only by becoming the husband? Is there no rule or ideology or tradition for the husband in a happy married life? The husband is free and the wife is captive. The wife shall keep sacrificing her entire life with her love and also be blamed. Why are there different rules for both, when both have taken birth in human form, their death is also certain, then why is there such a disparity of rules in the lifestyle? The woman creates, she gives birth by keeping the baby in her womb for 9 months and if she is not able to become a mother, then she is blamed. Is she merely a property or merely an object of consumption or an instrument of a man immersed in sensuality? She has to discover this truth, not by sacrificing her entire family along with her small child ruthlessly, but after performing her worldly duties. Sujata took the difficult decision of following this path of accomplishment in the latter part of her life. She took the initiation in a monastery in Saket from the son of God, Buddha. Having renounced all the opulence of her life, she became a great ascetic after conquering her desires. The maid's daughter Poornika also got attainment from the hands of Lord Buddha. ❑

Khemavati

In 600 BC,many big states located in the north-west of India used to send their messengers to other states in order to establish their power. Even in a vast state like Gandhar, there were many small and big republics. The country Gandharva is located on both sides of the beautiful vast sweet-water Indus River. This route of the Indus River was connected to the Meeni route of Magadha kingdom through Mansera Haripur valley. In its north-eastern part, there was a republic, Madra, which was situated in the valley of the five-river region. Fertile soil, immense kindness of the waters of the five rivers. Hence this state was extremely prosperous and developed. Due to Taxila University being a few miles away from here, the kings of Magadha, Anga, Kaushal all other countries wanted to come here and keep their contact with the republics. Coming from the eastern parts of India, when it seemed impossible to conquer the vast developed countries located so far away through war, they married their princesses and made their establishment. This is a diplomatic move. *Maharaja Pukkusati* of Gandhar also sent his messengers to Magadhraj Bimbisara. Magadhraj defeated the king of Anga region and expanded his kingdom from northeastern India to its south eastern borders. Now there is a desire to merge the Kaushal state. Thus, the proposal of marriage to the princess of Madra republic was sent through his messenger. Princess Kshema is very beautiful. Discussions of her beauty are everywhere. The speciality of women of Gandhar is that they are of very fair complexation. The pupils of their eyes have the blue aura of Lake Mansarovar. Long nose and sharp features always distinguish them from other women. Among thousands of rupees, she introduces herself as the full moon of the full moon night because of her radiant white skin and tall stature. Kshema is not only a beautiful princess but also a very intelligent and sensitive young woman.She is the favourite princess of her republic. Always waiting in the dreamland for her future prince. She has seen many scholars, princes, economists and politicians come to Taxila. Many of them accept hospitality in their republic before returning to their respective countries after the completion of their education. Because in Taxila it takes at least 12 years to get initiation of any subject. Not all refuse the king's request to be respected for hospitality after so many years of sojourn away from their homes. That is why the logical intelligence of Kshema has developed so much. If an intelligent girl gets the company of scholars, then think how much development would have happened in her remarkable intellect. Her aspirations regarding her future husband were also noble and high. The social practices that assess women with the strength of their husbands and the efforts to protect their kingdoms, gave birth to many such traditions in which the harm is done only to the women.

Princess Kshema, highly educated, very beautiful and very young was a victim of this tradition. Without her consent, she was married to the Magadha king Bimbisara so that her kingdom would be safe and could not be conquered by attacking foreign soldiers. Every republic considers it to be lucky to have relations with the Magadha kingdom because in future all kinds of security facilities will be available to it only from the vast states. And then princesses are born so that they are either married to those kings or they are presented with humiliation in post-war treaties. Princess Kshema was slightly lucky. She did not succumb to any war treaty, but married like a respected princess and became the queen of Magadha. She reached Magadha by sacrificing her education, etiquette, cultural policies, courage and dreams. She was given a grand welcome in Magadha. About 500 queens of Bimbisara were envious of seeing the beauty of Ksemavati. Kshemvati was accompanied by 80 maidservants. The people of Magadha were surprised to see the beauty of those maids. The intelligent maids started acting like spies as soon as they arrived. The innumerable queens of the *Maharaja (King)*, his blind love for the dancer and illegitimate child, prince Abhay, who was found in a dying state in the forest outside the borders of the state, and as soon as he took him on his lap, he started breathing and therefore he named him Jivak. All this news was gathered by the maids of Ksemavati and was conveyed to their princesses. This news is also not hidden that one of his sons, Ajatashatru, wants to get the throne very soon and for that he is planning various types of conspiracies. Like the other eminent princesses, Kshema too silently accepted her fate and looked forward to the night of her first meeting with her husband. Her maids decorated her with ornaments and silk garments according to the tradition of Gandhara. Specially arranged her long, golden hair. The entire bedroom was decorated with fragrant *Juhi* flowers. In every corner of the room, golden lamps were dimly lit, in which the beauty of Princess Kshema started shining like a golden goddess. Kshema was astonished to see this supernatural form of herself in front of a life-sized mirror. She eagerly waited for the arrival of the king. This was not the first marriage of the king of Magadha and he has always been associated with women. He had a lustful desire to go to Kshema, but he did not have the patience of a man of character. As soon as he reached the bedroom - he was astonished to see Kshema in this supernatural form. Standing before Kshema in front of a life-sized mirror, he started staring at her beauty. The blood flow in his arteries intensified. He started losing complete control over himself, but as soon as he saw his reflection in the mirror with that divine beautiful girl, he was shocked. Glimpses under a golden crown, dangling white hair strands, wrinkled face, sloping shoulders swaying out of such a beautiful silk robe appeared as if it was sighing at the arrival of old age.Seeing his mature form, the young man became ashamed in front of his wife. Ksemavati had also sensed the pain of youth passing away in the lost sight of the emperor. The Magadha emperor looked so disgusting and unbearable that the effigy of lust appeared in front of him. She said with a squid laugh - "O *Aryaputra*, you are welcome. I have come here from a faraway state. I am completely ignorant of the customs and food habits here. Give me some time and I feel suffocated in such a small palace. O *Aryaputra*, how can a young woman like me live in a closed room? Please make proper arrangements for my stay and my satisfaction." The blood flowing in the emperor's arteries suddenly became very cold. Even if he wanted to, he would not be able to satisfy this young woman, such a realization of his masculinity happened at that very moment. He thought of leaving soon, but before leaving he said to Kshema, "Dear you are a queen, a special queen. Your accommodation will be arranged in a huge palace very soon. That palace is in the north of *Venuvan* in our capital itself. A very beautiful garden will also be made for you. Live as per the choice of your style and tradition." Having said this, he left very quickly. Truthfully, a wise woman never attacks her enemy directly. She strikes his weakest side humbly, indirectly so that the enemy completely accepts his defeat and that's what happened. The emperor himself was defeated in front of Kshema. The egoistic man selected the most beautiful palace for Kshema and ordered the construction of the garden as promised. Princess Kshemawati is now Queen Kshema. Her womanhood is also defeated in this war. There is no lover of her beautiful body, pure mind, dreams and longings in her eyes. The queen has carved a compound rampart of pride, arrogance, rigidity and indifference around the fibres of her sharp intellect. No one can trespass it. Now she is busy only in grooming so that all the queens of Magadha get jealous of her beauty. All the queens will have to burn in the same fire, in which their body, mind and conscience are being destroyed. Kshema is now leading a luxurious life. Once or twice, at the behest of the king, she participated in the conference of scholars in the royal court. There she was astonished to hear wise women likeMaitreyi and Rohini. When Rohini translated Panini's grammar and explained it in simple *Pali*, then even Kshema could not remain without being impressed by it. How do these two wise women independently travel in the country and abroad? They promote education. They have completely memorized the mantras of *Vedas*. Her heart also wanted to participate and communicate with other scholars in such meetings, but the arrogant queen does not want to come out of the maze of lies of her lifestyle.

The king feels great regret about the state of Kshema but he is helpless. Daughter – in adulthood she is unable to satisfy a very handsome women's man. The emperor himself has become tired now. He no longer likes to battle. His very dear son also considers him his enemy. His secret lover, the royal dancer, has also turned away from him. His heart is deeply saddened. He meets Gurus of different sects for peace of mind but no one is successful in showing him the right path. In the desire for the expansion of his kingdom, he defeated Anga king and subjugated the kingdom of Anga. Able Naresh had married Prasenjit's sister only to get Kashi. Kaushala Devi was a very dear queen. But now again in old age, he married Vaishali Chetak's daughter Chellana. He used to keep Chellna with him. Chellna is also very intelligent. She knows how much respect is given to a wife brought in old age. She would live with the king like his shadow. Chellana was a follower of Jainism. The Adhir king did not get any peace even in Ajivak religion. Goshal, the original propagator of Ajivak religion, was also unable to guide him. Then queen Chellana very cleverly captivated him with her logic and knowledge and the Magadha emperor became a follower of Jainism. This was the biggest victory of queen Chellana. Now she had control over the whole of Magadha and the mind of the emperor. Then news came in Magadha that Lord Gautam Buddha was coming to the palace via Taxila. Emperor Bimbisara is always attracted to religious *gurus*. Without delay, he started preparations to welcome him. With benevolence, he humbly made arrangements for the accommodation of all the monks. A monastery was built for them in Jaitwan. Gautam Buddha came with his disciples and started giving discourses in the city. People of the kingdom were mesmerized by his discourses. Thousands of men and women started wishing for his *darshan*. The whole city was lost in the voice of Buddha. One day the king also told queen Kshema that "Buddha is coming to Venuvan. Your mind will get peace. Be sure to visit him. If possible, listen to the voice of Lord Buddha also. We will never get such a fortune again." Queen Kshema immediately refused. Slowly she realized that her maidservants go to listen to Buddha's discourses and surprisingly there is a change in their nature as well. They also looked down upon all the other women while enslaved to Queen Kshema. There was no decency in conduct. The arrogant maidens of the arrogant queen suddenly started treating everyone with utmost humility. A special kind of peace and aliphatic is reflected on their face. Queen Kshema also covers her face with a cloth, walks from her palace on foot and reaches Venuvan. There is a very peaceful atmosphere all around. Thousands of citizens are enchanted and are sitting in *Vinaya Mudra* in front of Buddha. Kshema also quietly takes her place in the last row and starts listening to Buddha's speech. Buddha's straight, pure vision falls on Queen Kshema. As if she is hypnotized. She feels that the whole universe is spinning – her present, past and future are beginning to flow in front of her eyes. The beauty she takes so much pride in is only momentary. She sees how breath-taking a beautiful girl child looks in her adolescence. When she attains full puberty in her youth, she becomes like a very beautiful angel. Then after a few years, heaviness comes into her body. Beauty remains but attractiveness starts diminishing. Slowly that beauty also starts to fade away. Now her body has bloated. The whole hair starts to scatter in different directions like white fibres of cotton. The evergreen white skin has started to loosen and hang. Like soil has been coated on the radiance of the face. The face has become wrinkled. The beautiful girl who used to walk stiffly, now her back has started to bend. All the teeth in the mouth are fallen. With her hollow mouth, sunken eyes, dreadfully ugly wrinkled face, a bent back, she suddenly fell into the mud while walking with her trembling legs. As soon as she becomes lifeless and become a part of the soil, thousands of small insects from the earth come out in a row moving forward and start eating her skin very quickly. Its stink is spread all around. No one is even touching her. Seeing such a horrifying form, Queen Kshema's mind started baffling. She fainted there and fell down. The monks informed her maidservants and they came and took her to the palace. As soon as Queen Kshema regained consciousness, she became unsteady, ran and stood in front of that huge mirror and started remembering her dream again. There was no angel in that mirror but she saw her reflection. Slowly all that started happening to her reflection that she had seen in the subconscious mind in the meeting of Gautam Buddha. "So, is this her future?" She looked at her maid with a questioning look. The maid understood the feelings of her mistress. Only a woman can understand the pain of another woman's mind without saying anything. She also said - "Yes mistress, this is the truth. This beauty of us is momentary. We are born again and again and die. To get rid of this cycle of life and death, we have to go on the path of spiritual practice.

Queen Kshema immediately leaves the palace and goes to Buddha. "Oh dear, show me the way. Will this life of mine just go in vain? For the welfare of society, for the welfare of humanity, show me the way. I will follow it completely. I want salvation *Bhante*, I want salvation. I want to be forgiven for all my mistakes, of transgressions, I want to improve, I want to repent. Hey bhante, please accept my request. Give me forgiveness, meditation, patience, peace, a guide to liberation." Lord Buddha said, "Kshema, do not blame yourself. Engage in the service of social and human welfare. From there you will get salvation."

The *Bhikshuni Sangha* was founded by the persuasion of Mahaprajapati Goutami. In course of time, from the royal dancer to the royal patron, Vishakha, Nagarvadhu and Vidushi Rohini, Vimalakriti, Dasi, Nanduttara, Kundalakesi all became nuns. The one who fed Tathagata kheer had also become an ascetic in the latter part of her life by renouncing her house and family. Queen Kshema also became the most respected teacher of the Sangh. She propagated the teachings of Buddhism in the country and abroad. Visited many places and built nunnery monasteries. To smoothly run the Bhikshuni Sangha a method of operation was established. She continued to serve Buddhism for the rest of her life and attained Nirvana. Kaushal Naresh was once a follower of Jainism, but after his three consecutive defeats, he became mentally very weak and his mind wandered around for peace.He also went to the refuge of Lord Buddha, but the questions and doubts hovering in his mind continued to stir him up. Then, showing a sharp intellect, *Bhikshuni Ksemavati*, demonstrating her philosophy in a very simple language, pacifies every curiosity and satisfied with the answers of Ksemavati, the majestic king Prasenjit becomes a follower of Buddha.

Prasenjit questions, "How will the experience of a Tathagata prosperous *Bodhisattva* be, who is alive till then or will he remain a *Bodhisattva* even after it?" Ksemavati very simply asks, "King now tell how many number of particles of sand are there under the flowing river, you are a master of mathematics, count it or tell the account of the drops of water in the ocean. Prasenjit then replied, "The river keeps on flowing, who can count the sand particles that live with it, and the bottomless ocean is limitless. It is impossible to calculate the number of drops and measure the depth of it." Then Ksemavati explained to him- "It is not necessary to calculate the sound, measure it in the cycle of life and death, or know where they were before birth, where they will go after death. Their existence has to be felt. We don't have to think about its beginning and end, it is the beginning and it is the end, how can you find its end?" Prasenjit then realized that he could attain nirvana only by taking refuge in the Lord. Ksemavati was not just a nun. Rather, she was a philosophical teacher and conductor of a high order. Kshemavati is the only queen whom Buddha himself initiated in the palace and all the women of the state became Buddhists with Ksemavati. On the strength of her subjects, Kshema spent the rest of her life in public welfare. Seeing her piety, Lord Buddha honoured her with the title of *"Mahaprajapati"*.

❑

Kundalkeshi

A woman's mind is full of emotions. She does not let anyone know what is going on in her conscience. Sometimes she is simple and easy-going by nature and sometimes she becomes gruff and stone-hearted in the face of adversity. Sometimes she spends her whole life being bound to her culture and traditions, and sometimes she challenges them by walking between those social beliefs. This story is of one such girl who, even after being very intelligent since childhood, takes all her life's decisions by the deep feelings of her heart.

The capital of the Magadha Empire is Rajagriha, where the king's huge empire has splendid palaces, exemplary pavements, exquisite gardens and huge buildings of royal staff. All this is inside the premises of *Raj Bhavan*. Bhadra is the only daughter of the resident *Shulkadipti* officer. She is very beautiful, but due to her logical intellect, she goes to the root cause of each event to know the cause. No one can defeat her in logic. She takes her own decisions. To some extent, she is a boisterous and obstinate youth. She likes to disregard the prevailing traditions of the social structure. She is a girl of very unique and independent thoughts from heart and mind. Her parents are very worried about this nature of hers. Because they anticipate that women having such thoughts in married life are often unhappy. They are somewhat apprehensive about the young girl's marriage and that she should not take any unpleasant step by getting carried away in her emotions. That's why they mostly keep her in the house and do not allow her to go out. They do not even imagine travelling with her. Bhadra loves nature very much. Natural beauty fascinates her. Lost in the same natural beauty, Bhadra keeps fantasizing about the first man to come into her life.

Once, after taking a bath, she was standing on the roof of her building to dry her beautiful long hair and then her sight fell on the way to the palace. She saw some of the king's soldiers tying the hands of a handsome man and leading him towards the open court of the palace. At first sight, Bhadra was impressed with the way the young man walked and his strong physique. She realized that this young man is not only very strong but courageous and sensitive as well. Not everyone has feelings. Insensitive people look like dead people to Bhadra. But many people express their feelings very cleverly and many are also adept at hiding those feelings. A woman of a simple nature like Bhadra herself gets entangled in the web of human sensibilities. It is never right to be insensitive, but to flow into them without thinking is a sign of gross stupidity. Bhadra too, flowing in the impulse of feelings rising in her heart starts wandering in the imaginary world that believes easily in everyone and falls in love at first sight with that young man, who believes easily in everyone. The harsh surface of reality has not yet been faced. She is very dear to her parents, she has not experienced different forms, times or seasons of life. Bhadra is ignorant of the consequences of her invisible future. The young man is a perfect thief, but he is full of morale. Where ordinary people tremble with fear at the sight of soldiers. How confident is this thief walking? Bhadra was impressed by his fearless man. The young man also looked around while going and immediately saw the thoughtless teenager, drying her wet hair waving on the roof of the building of Shulkadipti. There is no need for any communication or medium of language to express love. The feelings of love are exchanged through the eyes. First sight of first love in that auspicious hour of the morning. The residences of the royal courtiers and officials of the monarchy are located inside the premises of the palace itself. Bhadra's father is a highly educated, elite and soft-spoken officer. It is his primary duty to collect taxes for the state. Being very wealthy and respected, he directly intervenes in other activities that take place in the palace. Bhadra's mother is very simple-natured but has no control over her daughter's mind. Bhadra made up her mind to marry the same young man. The constrained parents explained to her a lot, even threatened her a little and in the end, wept for their honour. Nothing is acceptable to stubborn Bhadra.

It is the law of nature that the person who rules the world is ultimately defeated by his children. Shulkadipti is helpless in front of his only dear daughter. The youth is accused of theft. Punishment has not been given yet. He will be punished only after considering both sides in the royal court. There is also the possibility of him being innocent in the end. Assuming this, Shulkadipti prayed to the king. The young man is the son of a Brahmin. He is making a living through misdeeds like stealing. Anyway, *Brahmins* are seen with respect in society. Even a hundred of their faults are forgiven or ignored. The young man, being a Brahmin by birth, is pardoned even while committing execrable jobs, and he readily accepts the proposal of marrying that girl so that he can be freed from the crime of stealing with a sceptre in future. The saddened couple marries their only daughter to that Brahmin youth. In a chariot, dressed in diamond-ruby ornaments and silk robes, Bhadra enters the heart of her husband. The young woman, who was immersed in the feelings of the mind wandering in the world of imagination, has now become the housewife in the *Grahasth ashram*. A girl who adopts first love, at first sight, has a blind belief on her husband. She finds him the most unique, handsome, sensitive man in the world. The husband is *brahmin* only by birth but is a sly, robber and treacherous by action. He loves his wife but loves her jewellery and wealth way more than that.

In the first year of married life, the greedy husband took advantage of his beautiful teenage wife. When his craving began to dissipate from the attraction of his wife, then there was a fascination with her ornaments. Now in his mind, he quickly started planning to get rid of his wife. He knows that if he abandons his wife, his father-in-law will give him the sceptre. That is why he started making plans to take his wife's life forever so that he would get all the ornaments and also freedom from married life. One night, while lying beside his wife in the bedroom, he said with great affection, "Dear, you have brought so much happiness and satisfaction to my life. We will always live like this and do some virtuous work for our future children. But I am still not free from sceptre. That is why I have made a vow to Goddess Nilgiri that I will make a golden idol and establish it. Last night, Goddess Nilgiricame in my dream and blessed me. Dear, give me all your jewellery and money so that after selling it, I can make a gold idol from a goldsmith and establish it on the mountain and get the blessings of freedom from punishment. Both of us will go to that peak next week on the auspicious day of *Akshaya*

Tritiya and will complete this work methodically. Goddess will fulfill all your wishes."

The naive, contented, unshakable wife immediately handed over all her jewellery to the husband. A woman considers her husband as her true jewel. She does not compare the love of her husband to diamonds and rubies. As planned, both started the journey a week before *Akshaya Tritiya*. The wife wants to go in her palanquin. Her father also has made arrangements for horses, but the sly husband wants to take his wife to the mountain ranges in a very mysterious way. When going by horse or palanquin, slaves will also have to be taken along. A terrible planning cycle is going on in his mind. He does not want to take anyone along with him on the journey. "Dear, for the fulfillment of the wish, we have to travel by ourselves and get blessings by having be *darshan* of the mountain goddess." Saying such false words, he convinced his wife to go alone on the journey. The wife is also very happy. She is going on a travel to a pilgrimage with her life partner after one year of her marriage. The couple reached the forest, crossing the zig-zag paths of the sub-divisions, crossing the highway, carrying some materials and all the ornaments for the couple's route in a box. This journey is very sweet for Bhadra. Living alone with her loving husband and the vision of a bright future is making her journey very captivating. At night they camped in a cave in the mountain. In the morning, the husband said, "Give me all the ornaments. We will offer it to the goddess, then go to the city and get its idol made by a goldsmith and establish it." Bhadra handed over all her jewellery to her husband with utmost devotion and respect. Holding her husband's hand, she started climbing the mountain. Holding the chest full of ornaments in one hand and the wife's hand in the other, the husband slowly began to climb the rock. As soon as he started pushing Bhadra, at that very moment Bhadra's eyes fell on him. She hurriedly backed down to save her life. Unexpectedly in an instant, the husband's balance got disturbed. Because in one hand was a box of ornaments. He fell into a deep gorge on the other side of the rock with that box. Immediately the goddess of death takes him in her shelter. What can be sadder for a wife than that the husband whom she loves and trusts more than her life, will betray her so fiercely. Her heart is so traumatized that she does not mourn the death of her husband. But she is sad that her loving husband tried to take her life for some jewellery. Even if that greedy husband had requested her for all the ornaments, she would have easily given away all her wealth and jewellery. If he would have specifically told that he is bored by the craving for his wife's body, Bhadra herself would have gone out of his way and abandoned him. But seeing such a terrible conspiracy involving greed and hatred, she is unable to come back to normalcy. On the other hand, she wandered like mad on the mountain and kept doing self-examination. Somewhere inside, all the feelings in her heart have now dried up. She started wandering here and there after getting distracted to achieve the goal of her meaningless life. Returning to the city again, she did not go to the shelter of her parents. She has started hating even worldly life. Married life has started seeming like a sin to her.

At that time *Shasvat Muni* used to propagate *Dharma*. The worshiper of non-violence, the originator of Jainism, who showed the way to get rid of the cycle of life and death, did not believe in casteism or tribe. His followers were all men and women. Bhadra reached Pavapuri while wandering. She took refuge in the ashram of Tirthankara and was influenced by his speech and took initiation in

Jainism. In Jainism, women are allowed to live in the ashram. They have to wear white clothes. Vegetarian food is to be consumed only twice before sunset. She will abandon all the rules of the *grihasth ashram*. She will always spend her whole life in the defence of religion only then will she become a *Sadhvi*. Now she has become a woman *Sadhvi*. She chopped off her black hair. According to Jain tradition, each hair is uprooted and separated. This process is very painful so that the hair does not grow again, it is uprooted from the root itself. In this process, the whole head bleeds, but the *Sadhvi* happily accepts to bear this pain. For some time lived in the ashram as a *Sadhvi*, studying *Dharma, Vedas, Puranas and* scriptures. Participated in *Dharma* meetings, carried on discussions, but her mind could not find peace anywhere. With time, beautiful hair began to grow on her head again. Curly thick black hair started growing in a coiled manner. Now everyone started calling *Sadhvi* by the name of Kundalkeshi. Kundalkeshi would boldly argue about religion with the gurus of Jainism, and when she did not get the answers to her questions, she started wandering impatiently. One day she took a decision and left Jainism and roamed from city to city and started participating in religious meetings. The ability to defeat beautiful Kundalkeshi is not in the power of any *Shastra guru*, priest, sage or discriminator. Everyone is defeated by her and some do not even want to argue because it becomes a state of great shame to be defeated by a woman.

Kundalkeshi is a winner now, no one shows the courage to defeat her in an argument. Her heart finds great joy in defeating the male society. But still, she did not get the path of truth. She used to often ask herself in solitude whether her life would end before knowing the truth. All my studies, my knowledge will go in vain. Will I never attain salvation? One day she planted a *Jambafal* plant in a sand dune outside the city and said that those who have the courage to criticize or argue with me can come here and invite her by plucking a branch of this tree. *Pundits* and scholars of different religions silently began to see that plant grow into a tree. One day monk Sauriputra came there. All the scholars requested him that only you can defeat Kundalkeshi. Sauriputra himself is a scholar. Very dear disciple of Lord Tathagata, very gentle and does not wish to defeat anyone. He is free from cravings. He does not aspire for any kind of award, title or glory. He does not want to humiliate a learned woman by defeating her in an argument. Then Kundalkaishi says, "Hey monk, you wander from city to city carrying alms, how can you answer my questions"? "Hearing this, Sauriputra humbly says – Oh Goddess, ask what you want to ask?" Kundalkeshi pours out all the knowledge acquired in her life in front of him, asking questions on each subject. With great patience and humility, Sauriputrakeeps answering. All the townspeople slowly start gathering in the meeting. Everyone listens and is mesmerizedby the explanation of religion, logic of both of them. Respectively the day started passing by and at the end, Kundalkeshi had no more questions to ask. Then she says to Sauriputra, "Now you ask me your questions. Sauriputra replies the secret of Divine life is never found in questions and answers. You can get it only by following a difficult sadhana path. Still, Kundalakeshi said arrogantly, "Monk at least ask me a question. The monk asked, "Who is that one on whom the whole life's force is determined." Now the answer to this simple and direct question cannot be either the creator or God. Kundalkeshi remembered all her knowledge, but unanswered, evening time is passing. All the townspeople forgetting their work are waiting for the answer to the question from Kundalkeshi. Sauriputra said, "It is food," which gives us the power to keep our life alive. The strength in the body gives strength to the mind and the mind is of foremost importance in all the ideologies of our life. Hearing his answer, Kundalkeshi came to know that, the teacher, the *guru* for whom she was wandering all her life, is this *guru*. She accepts her defeat. Her image has been shattered. She bows down at the feet of Sauriputra and requests him. "O monk, take me under your shelter, make me a disciple, give initiation." Sauriputra is soft-spoken and reticent. He only replies, "O woman, my Guru is Lord Buddha, the guide of me and the whole world. You take refuge in him." Kundalakeshi follows Sauriputra. Arrive at Jaitwan Vihar. Seeing such a serene and calm environment there, her mind becomes calm. Hundreds of nuns are reciting *Sutta*. All her ego, arrogance, pride, everything gets absorbed in the soil. She considers herself endless, insignificant in front of them all. That is when Buddha is seen coming. All the people present there were immersed in the nectar rain that freed them from bondage. Lord Buddha was doing *Dhamma-Desana* sitting under a tree. Kundalkeshi was greatly impressed by seeing his calm, beautiful and impressionable face. She had never seen such a sun-like form before. Kundalkeshi is well versed in scriptures. She saw *Mahamuni Buddha's* seat made of *Trinamool*. She was astonished to see the footprints of Buddha. She is also a complete knower of body characteristics. She saw that the feet of *Bhante* were crossed. Such a person is completely free from worldly attachments and illusions. That person is free from the bondage of anger, aversion and web of emotions. He is a great man. Kundalkeshi's mind became calm after listening to the welfare discourses of *Samyak Sambuddha*. The real vision of the *Bodhisattva*, the pragma in the form of peace, becomes known to her consciousness at that very moment. She experiences the truth. She gives up all the pitfalls of her life. Now there is no animosity towards anyone. There is no hope of going into any victory or defeat process. There is no craving to get anything, only to walk on the path of truth, to be qualified. Nirvana is to be attained. Kundalkeshi's journey of life comes to rest in the shelter of Lord Buddha. In the last phase of her life, Kundalkeshi gains fame as an eminent *Agrasevika*. The *bhikshuni* attains nirvana while performing her duties as the best teacher of the *Sangha*.

❏

Amrapali

The selection of a royal dancer is a social and state festival. This ritual is not celebrated every year, but in the year in which there is an extra month, that year Vaishali city is decorated like a bride and in the spring festival residents of the city get together in the porch of the palace and in Vaishali city, the king announces a new royal dancer that year, on the same day she is given the title of the royal dancer in front of all the subjects and she sits in the highest seat of the state. Far from the reach of common people, even the family members of the royal family, rulers, generals etc. are unable to meet her. The royal dancer is allotted a special palace to live in. Until another royal dancer is appointed, she rules alone. The special facilities given to the queen by the state, also have right to it. In her service 120 courtesans, dancers, centenarians and 100 maids are appointed for her beauty services. Young girls from vast developed cities like Kaushambi, Pataliputra, Avantpuri do hard work and penance to become a royal dancer. Well, which woman would not want to get so much opulence and respect, but the process of getting this respect is as complicated and difficult as the life of a royal dancer. At the onset of the Ashwin month, the search for a future roral dancer begins in every village and town. First rule: Girl should not be menstruating, that is, less than 11 years of age. She should be beautiful, soft-spoken and proficient in music and dance. Preference is given to girls of higher caste. They are selected by the king himself, his special counsellors and the Northeast politicians. His decision is final. Sometimes this interval is of 8 years and sometimes of 12 or 16 years. One extra *Ashadha* month comes in 10 years. In the atmosphere of *Vasant Panchami* of the same year, the royal dancer is announced amidst new blooming flowers.

A girl child was born to Tript Dev in an Ansuya village of Licchavi region. In summer, his wife went to the mango forest and gave birth to that girl. The mother believed a lot in worship, was extremely kind in nature and full of compassion. When that girl was born, the mangoes were ripening sweet, the cuckoo was singing in the Ambu forest. There was a musical atmosphere all around. The mother was feeling less of her labour pain by the cuckoo's singing. When the beautiful girl was born, her father named her Amrapali and lovingly called her Amba or Ambapali. She was kind, soft-spoken and very beautiful like her mother. At the age of 11 itself, she was taking classical music and dance lessons from the priest of her village deity. According to tradition she was selected and she had to come to Vaishali leaving her parents behind. There she was declared a royal dancer after winning a competition from about 1000 beautiful girls. When King Bimbisara himself saw her for the first time, he fell in love with her in his heart. Despite being so mighty and having many queens, the king's heart started feeling youthful again after seeing Amrapali. Many of his sons were now young and some were even married, but men do not have control of sexuality and lust. When the feudal lord had dedicated his daughter to the kingdom, then the princes of many small and big kingdoms were ready to even fight to get her, who would not want to get such a unique beauty. To give her a special title did not mean to respect her, but it was that fine flexible strong net of the hunter, in which the prey remains trapped forever and can never be free in the living state. Amrapali was given a special state palace to live in and in-front of her was a very beautiful garden. The king asked Amrapali in private, how is it feeling here? Amrapali said humbly, there is a lot of opulence here, I also have special arrangements for music and dance, but I want that mango forest of my village. If you make arrangements for that, I will always be grateful to you. Bimbisara was blown away in his heart, what a naive young woman, immersed in simplicity. The king immediately ordered to convert the flower forest of Vaishali city into a mango forest. As soon as the order was received, the gardeners of the state started making a beautiful and huge mango forest. But nature runs on its own time. It took 5 years for the mango forest to fully bloom, in those 5 years, Amrapali also blossomed as a beautiful gentle dancer. Discussions of her beauty started happening all around, the richest of the rich became eager to lay down everything on her, that simple Amrapali was now shattered by the beauty of her appearance and status. She had the knowledge that this life is not permanent, in the next few years a new royal dancer would be appointed, but somewhere in her mind, this belief had settled that no one could replace her and that she would make the monarchy work as she wanted. If possible, she will stop the process of appointment of a royal dancer forever and spend her whole life as a dancer. Craving and glamour's strange game began. The prey herself begins to think that she has caught the hunter in her net and is obliged to accept her possession. In the kingdom of feudal lords, a woman was only a material of consumption and when the same consuming animal gets so much respect, then its mental balance is ought to be disturbed a little bit. Amrapali started living in luxury with her maids. She looked down upon the other townspeople of her state, while prostitution was also acceptable in the society. Special arrangements were made for them in the city, but people full of lust used to go to them only to satisfy their physical hunger. They could not imagine reaching Amrapali even in their dreams. Many princes and wealthy businessmen would camp outside her palace and sit in the camp so that they might have a sight of her sometime. Only those who had the ability to launder immense wealth could reach her through discussions of her music and dance. Even the eyes of Ajatashatru, the very dear son of King Bimbisara, had fallen on Amrapali. He too was making various efforts to get her. Amrapali had some human qualities, giving to the needy, respecting the *sannyasis* but in the pride of her beauty and royal status, those feelings had gotten buried somewhere. There were occasions in this cycle of life when she also had to be in a compromising position with *Mahabalis*, when the king himself came to her bedroom at night, she was delighted at the moment of orphaned happiness. She felt that she was the queen of Vaishali, the mature king did not want to make a mistake in showing the emphasis of his masculinity and above all the intoxication of the beauty of Amrapali. He stayed in her palace for a week and kept mating with her completely like a thirsty whirlpool. This news reached Prince Ajatashatru as well, he too decided in his heart that one day he would make love with Amrapali. After the king left, Amrapali's nature started to change, now she started behaving like an arrogant queen. Earlier sometimes she used to meet brides of Vimalakriti Padmavati Nagar, but now she had started to feel that these women were of low nature. Seasons changed and the seeds of male sexuality began to grow in Amrapali's womb. According to tradition, brides of the city and royal dancers did not have the right to give birth to children, also no father gives their name to the child. The ruthless society bound by the policies of patriarchy does not accept children born out of contact without marriage at any cost. Amrapali was also no different, the king had got her and it was written in her destiny to become the mistress of everyone else.A simple prostitute showed her position while she was walking in the garden hiding her womb. There is no difference between you and me, Amrapali, you will never be able to give a father's name to this unborn child, both of us are sold in this flesh trade market. We are judged by our condition but you will never be able to get the happiness of motherhood and it is not that all the men on earth will be crazy about your beauty. There will be some on whom the magic of your beauty will not work on. She went away and Amrapali felt as if she has fallen from dreamland to the ground. The same thing happened, she could not muster the courage to renounce the title of a royal dancer, her mind, brain and consciousness were so clogged by opulence that she had deprived her of intelligence that she sacrificed the happiness of motherhood. The maidservants wrapped her first child in a silk cloth and left her on the side of a deserted road in the dark night. The milk flowing from her chest became a lump, giving her physical as well as mental pain, and sweet talks of princes, soothing dreams, tempting rewards did not pacify but she herself wanted a life like this. In life, we only get according to the variety of wants we have in our conscious and subconscious mind. Some of the maids show sympathy to her condition and some pass squid smiles behind her back. Both the circumstances are not hidden from her. She is helpless and in great pain, this helplessness has made her angry and obstinate, now she makes her lovers dance to her tunes, plays with their hearts, cuddles and scolds. The passionate lovers of her youth wait for her approval like pet dogs. This time too Vaishali was busy preparing for the arrival of spring, the arrival of spring was feeding a wonderful shade of joy in everyone's mind, nature had become youthful. The buds were slowly starting to bloom on the shivering plants buried during winter. All the animals and birds were welcoming the spring with joy, the Sumera river flowing outside the city is in its splendour. The natural beauty of the mountain foothills is at its puberty with the advent of spring, the *Basant* festival is observed not for a day but for the whole week, the towns brides who live in the traditional household also decorate their workshops beautifully. She can never bind or marry in any family bond, but arrangements for the accommodation of her relatives and maids are also made especially outside each city. Whenever there is a music or dance festival, it is inaugurated by a royal dancer. This prestige and divine honour have been bestowed upon a royal dancer. All classical music gurus want to start each of their programs with a royal dancer, that is why Amrapali becomes very busy with the onset of spring. High stature, long curly black hair, slender long fingers playing on the *Mrignayani sitar*, complexation of a white lotus and a face glowing with confidence. All music lovers, entertainment lovers are able to see her publicly every year during this season. There is a wave of joy all around, to see the dance of Amrapali, *Avantika Puri Pava*, princes from Shri Rampuri and wealthy people are reaching Vaishali from far away. Their wives also do not envy Amrapali because they know that their husbands go only for entertainment, no one can describe Amrapali and give her the status of a wife in a household. Then *Maharaj* got the news that Lord Buddha himself was coming to Vaishali city with his monks, he would rest for a week on the hill located outside the city and give discourses to his followers. People who are willing will be made monks, now in a moment, the spring atmosphere, full of pomp, has become very devotional. The king ordered that every citizen should get involved in welcoming Lord Buddha. The king himself is a follower of Jainism, wandered for a few days in his lifelong religion, but his mind could not find complete peace anywhere. He wanted to meet Lord Buddha since a long time, it is his good fortune that this year *Bhante* himself is visiting his kingdom. The *pandals* that were built for entertainment all over the state are now decorated with flowers. There were sitting arrangements made for the monks and after removing all the musical instruments, only a beautiful simple meeting was arranged. The whole city became devotional, there was a competition among the princes to invite Buddha, but permission would have to be taken from Ananda, the dearest disciple of Lord Buddha before anything else. Amrapali also started thinking what kind of life is this, those who were longing to have a glimpse of me, suddenly are turning their backs and going to the refuge of Lord Buddha. I too have to take refuge in him, what is there in this life cycle? She also got her chariot ready and started going to the hill outside the city with her charioteer. The princes' who used to rebel against the family to get her, want to reach Lord Buddha first in a chariot race with her today.

When Amrapali reached the resting place, she saw thousands of people bowing their heads to Lord Buddha. All the buried humanity of her heart was suddenly awakened. She fell directly at the feet of Lord Buddha and started crying, requesting him to have food at her home. Lord Buddha replied calmly, I will definitely come to your house to take alms. Everyone was surprised that Lord Buddha will go to a royal dancer's house. The princes also made a humble request, please come to our palace, bless us. Lord Buddha said, we are monks, we have given a promise to Amrapali, tomorrow morning we will have food there before noon at her place, you request her. The prince said that Amrapali half Vaishali will be given to you, give us permission for tomorrow's meal. Amrapali had lost her greed for Aishwarya, she had come here to find her own existence. She replied, even if you give half the whole Vaishali, I will not accept it. I will only serve Lord Buddha.

Seeing her determined power of pledge, the *Bodhisattva* remained silent. When he went to her for a meal, Amrapali gave her property in alms to him and said God, I donate this in your service. You can establish a union here. Buddha monks accept everything that is donated, his disciple Ananda asked Bhante, a royal dancer wants to join the *sangha* by donating repeatedly. Buddha remained silent; everyone knows that to meet Buddha one has to take permission from Ananda. Ananda asked, *Bhante* she comes to me again and again, requesting to meet you, what should I do? *Bhante* said, you don't reply to her, don't even see her. Lord Buddha knew that Ananda was his dearest disciple.

Till now he has not got *Arharat*. He should not get lost in the beauty of Amrapali. Ananda also followed his Lord Buddha. No matter how much Amrapali tried to join the Sangh and talk to him, he turned his face with the same harshness and walked away silently, never looking at her even with a single glance. It was time for Lord Buddha to go back, having blessed his followers, he is going to take some youths with him by donating rags. Anand is following his every order flawlessly. When a woman is defeated from everywhere, then she shows her special character, Amrapali fell unconscious at the feet of Lord Buddha, Lord Buddha affectionately put his hand on her forehead and went ahead. She looked impatiently at Ananda who lives like a shadow with Lord Buddha but he did not attain *Bodhi*. Even though he is an ordinary man he is not looking at her. He had asked Lord Buddha that what should I do if someone comes in the way of *Dharma*? Bhante said that you should walk on the path of *Dharma* with restraint, if the world creates any obstacle, then never resist, do not give any answer and move towards your direction. If a progressive disciple is only following the words of his guru, people are following him, the paved highway looks like an ocean of devotees. Lord Buddha is being hailed all around. Amrapali leaves her palace and starts following Buddha. Amrapali is very proud of her aesthetic skills, numerous great ruling princes yearn to have a glimpse of her. King Bimbisara is ready to fight with anyone just by the sign of her eyes. When Amrapali asked permission to meet Lord Buddha, she was told that Ananda was his chief loyal disciple and without his approval nothing could happen. Buddha himself has praised the human qualities of Amrapali, then Ananda is only a disciple. How could he not allow that? In this confusion, Amrapali came to meet Ananda, but Ananda only followed the words of his guru. When Amrapali appeared before him, Ananda turned his face, not even once looking at her. Amrapali went on talking about her proposal, but even after listening to her melodious voice, Ananda did not reply to her. He silently stood unmoved. Amrapali had never been insulted like this before in her life, after being hurt in a defeated conscience, she returned to her *Raj Bhavan*. She started looking out of the window of her room, many *Seths* and Princes are sitting in their camps waiting to get her. She is the most respected and influential woman in the royal court of Vaishali city, but it did not have any effect on even a monk. Surely, he must have heard the description of her beauty, but didn't he ever have a craving to see her even for a moment? This same thing continued to strike Amrapali in her mind at every moment, the pride of her beauty started talking to herself. To her, herbeauty and her dance talent started seeming meaningless. If a man whose disciple is so controlled and loyal, then how knowledgeable must be his teacher. Only he can find the truth in her meaningless greedy life and be a pathfinder for her. Ananda's disdain for her indifference to her compels her to look within her soul. She wants to have various kinds of discussions with Ananda separately but she has no influence on Ananda. Amrapali gets frustrated seeing herself being defeated in every field, she no longer finds this wealth, opulence, standards of appreciation or status of a royal dancer, nothing interests her. A beautiful female body that is unable to attract an ordinary disciple wearing a rag, how can she be proud of the beauty of such a mortal body? It is the same Ananda who, staying in favour of *Maha Prajapati Goutami* in Kapilvastu, proposed for the entry of women in the *Bhante Sangha*. It is this disciple who believes in the right of respect for women and tries that the willing women in the society should also get the *pravjaya*. But he refuses to see my face and does not even talk to me. Does he not know about my sovereignty? Does he not know what a special woman Amrapali is? This question repeatedly hurts her soul. A disciple was not enchanted by her beauty, her talent, all the lovers of her beauty are leaving her and going to the refuge of Buddha, the crowd is pushing her and moving forward. Her pain, beauty, everything is getting mixed in the dust. How insignificant she has become in front of devotees. Men and women complement each other and give birth to new children, then is that all false? Appearance, beauty and charm will all become a part of the soil. Then what is the truth, Amrapali starts feeling guilty for herself. She is lying on the paved highway; people are passing by without looking at her. They are walking behind Lord Buddha, at that very moment Amrapali's inner soul cried out, Amba, it is the truth that you yourself have to adopt the path to get rid of the cycle of life and death. This delusion, opulence, attractiveness and brilliance of a beautiful body, everything is momentary, false. Break the shackles of this false dream and go in search of truth. Amrapali gets up slowly, now there is no anger, doubt, attachment or longing for anyone in her mind. Her mind has become stable, she also starts taking steps towards Lord Buddha with a calm mind. Amrapali shaved her hair and became a nun. The first nunnery union was established in Amravan, her establishing a nunnery is a historical event. There was a lot of rebellion in the society but it was a revolutionary decision. After that Vimala's work, Padmavati Maitri and many towns bride also took refuge in Buddhism and stayed in the *bhikshuni Sangha*. In a village situated on the banks of the Kali River, Buddha stayed at the behest of his dearest disciple Ananda. There was a restriction on the wisdom of women even in *Sankash Satsang*, they lifted that restriction and by giving initiation to *Alpa Swarna*, the door of Buddhism was opened for women. Earlier, the *bhikshuni* used to live in a separate hut in the city, but due to the anti-social elements in the society, arrangements were made for her to live in a separate union near the city. The nectar words of Buddha are always remembered, feeling of friendship towards all beings, compassion towards the afflicted and respect towards all beings of the world should be maintained. Keeping life pure by the means of the body, word and mind is *Dharma*, it was only after this preaching that the sprout of *Dharma* was developed in Amrapali's mind. Amrapali has recognized the truth of the impermanence of life in her inner self through spiritual practice in the form of a *bhikshuni*.

❑

Mallika

Human beings always use songs in times of war, festivals, prayer, happiness or sorrow. Songs, vocals and rhythm make up a beautiful composition of rhythmic words. Singing is such an art that every human being likes but not everyone can sing. Some craftsmen can sing beautiful songs by working hard, while some fortunate human beings are blessed by nature. Like a cuckoo dwell in their throat. Blessings of a sweet voice do not see any caste, religion, class, *varna* or age. Very few people are endowed with such blessings of the Lord.

Mallika is the only daughter of the front servant of the state. She is very dear to her father. There is so much sweetness in her throat that it is as if by squeezing the juice of sugarcane, it has moistened itself. Her nature is as sweet as her melodious singing. Very kind, compassionate and soft-spoken. Once Mallika filled her basket with food and fruits and went for a walk in the garden along with her friends. They were playing here and there like independent butterflies squabbling with each other spending the whole day in the garden. As soon as she sits down to eat, Mallika's eyes fall on some monks carrying alms on the road outside the garden and she realises that she should also donate food to them. Without a moment's delay, she takes her basket and reaches out to those monks, putting all the food with her into the vessel of the chief monk, bowing to all the monks, returns to her friends again. The chief monk smiles softly. His disciples want to know the secret of *Bhante's* smile because *Bhante* does not smile without a reason. Looking at his disciples, he says - "This girl will one day become the queen of this kingdom." His blessings are only for that girl. Disciple Upali asks - "O *Bhante*. How would that be possible? This girl is from a very simple family. By caste, she is not a *Kshatriya*. In royal families, marriages take place only in the caste system and with state relatives. Even the beauty of this compassionate woman is not so unique or attractive that the king should accept her. How will this be possible?" - *Bhante* remains silent and starts accepting the donation of the alms pot with a smile. The disciples know that their *Guru's* blessings are the truth. Everyone takes the food and proceeds to their monastery. With great joy, she has donated all her food items. She is satisfied by taking only a small portion of food and fruits from her friends. Slowly she starts humming a song. Before evening, she went to her abode with all her friends. She lives contentedly with her father in his small house.

The four major republics in the Middle Ages of the 6th BC are Vatsa, Magadha, Avanti and Kosala. Their kings keep on fighting with each other for their sense of ability. All the kings are busy fighting with each other and defeating other's kingdoms and increasing their empires. *Maharaja* Prasenjit is the majestic and mighty king of the Kaushal kingdom. He fought with the king of Anga and was defeated. Later, after the war with the Magadha king, his sister Kaushala Devi had to be married to Magadha king Bimbsar and along with one lakh gold coins in dowry had to be given to the city of "Kashi", but according to the treaty, he married the sister of Magadha king andsaved his rights. Kaushala Devi gave birth to Ajatashatru. Prasenjit again prepared for war and marched on Vatsaraja and was defeated. He was returning to his capital with his army after being very sad, then he started walking towards a garden alone. His mind is very disturbed. He is unable to stay steady anywhere. Only then he hears the voice of a very sweet song. A girl is singing a beautiful song to her own tune. Her voice is so clear and the lyrics are so sweet that Prasenjit forgets all his mental torture and starts listening to her, as soon as the song ends, he stands in front of the girl on his horse. The courageous girl without any fear of holding the reins, asks the king for his introduction, the king introduces himself to her and starts crying, narrating the agony of his defeat. The soft-spoken girl listens to him with utmost sensitivity and consoles him by gently wiping his tears. No matter how mighty a man may be, after defeat, when he breaks from within, he surrenders by going to the woman's lap. The king completely surrenders to the girl. He needs such a woman in his royal palace, with whom he can share his sorrows. Although Prasenjit has many queens, they all are busy in the splendour and opulence of the state. Immediately he proposes marriage to the girl. The girl also has no objection but she requests the king to take approval from her father. According to tradition, the king goes to her father's house with a courtship request and accepts Mallika as his wife and makes her the queen of Kaushalraj. Mallika follows Buddha's teachings even while staying in the royal palace. When she looks at the beautiful queens, dancers, city brides and maidservants around her, then the question comes to her mind that why everyone's fate and situations are different? She appears in the monastery of Buddha and asks Buddha one day - "Lord, some women are very virtuous and beautiful, then some are only virtuous and rich, then some are of the ordinary family but are full of qualities, then some women are neithervirtuous nor beautiful nor rich but live in different situations from each other. Someone is a ruler, and someone is a maid, why does this happen? Buddha, while resolving this doubt arising in the mind of the merciful naive Mallika, says - Man is subject to his actions, he keeps on committing sins every time to keep himself happy, such as carnal sins, killing, stealing and indulging in adultery. The second type of sin is a verbal sin like speaking false words but indulging in slander, speaking harsh words or speaking in vain and destroying one's *sattvik* power. Apart from this, there is another sin which is the most dreadful and makes us its slaves, that is mental sin, to covet, that is, covetousness by not being satisfied with what we have got - to act in greed, to hate, to be jealous means always comparing one's position to others, envying one who is more capable than oneself and finding fault with the *Tatva Gyan*". This discourse of his touched Mallika's heart. From queens to maidservants Mallika respects all. For any reason, she does not speak false words, the second queen gave birth to a son and Mallika gave birth to a girl, but she did not have any jealousy but happily nurtured her child "Vajira", she felt affectionate towards other princes. Does not covet any work or ability of the royal palace. Due to these qualities, queen Mallika had become very dear to the subjects. To the *Kshatrani* queens, this nature of her used to prick their eyes. Indulging in the greed of opulence, they looked down upon Mallika's beautiful nature, serene mind and simple life. Prasenjit made Mallika his queen in a weak moment of emotion, but he himself is a defeated warrior. Inferiority has made a home in his mind. He cannot remain calm and satisfied for long under any circumstances. He starts indulging in as many ritualistic activities as *Rajguru*, *Pandit* gives him advice.

King Prasenjit sometimes gets angry with queen Mallika. Says in harsh words - "You are the daughter of a simple family, you do not know the rules of the royal family, to fight, to expand the kingdom is the ultimate and first duty of the king". Hearing such harsh words from her husband, Mallika's mind is deeply hurt. No self-respecting woman would ever tolerate a comparison of the condition of her father's house with condemnation. Queen Mallika lives in the royal palace but she is not interested in this splendour. She is vehemently opposed to violence in animal sacrifice. She cannot even see her husband going on such a sinful path. That is why in many ways and with her logic, she keeps trying to change the mind of the king. Ajatashatru, the son of Prasenjit's sister, is forbidden to take control of the kingdom at a very young age and in order to get the kingdom, he imprisons his father. When his father dies, everyone calls him a "father killer". In this grief, his mother Kaushala Devi also passes away, due to which he becomes very sad. He takes an army and attacks Magadha but is defeated. After three consecutive defeats, Prasenjit becomes depressed. He is unable to concentrate. An amateur child, an unborn enemy defeated him, he could not bear it. The thought of committing suicide comes to his mind. At that time, it is Mallika who explains to her husband. She takes her husband in the shelter of Buddha. She explains Buddha's words to him - "Dear husband, you have been defeated thrice, do not try to win in vain. Winning creates enmity, the enemy will attack you and defeat you. This cycle of victory and defeat will never end. You listen to the discourse of Lord Buddha. He says each and every thing thrice so that even a foolish person can understand one thing in three times. You have been defeated thrice. There is nothing in war and victory. Finally, Prasenjit understands the meaning of the words of the queen.

Once earlier also Queen Mallika had opposed the violent sacrifice with her compassionate heart. Then Lord Buddha was residing in the Jaitavan monastery. Mallika took him to the monastery with great insistence. There Buddha explained to the king - "O king, a person who performs a violent *yajna* commits three kinds of misdeeds. The first is mental misdeeds by which he resolves to kill, the second is verbal in which he orders the murderer to murder. Third is physical misdeed in which he kills the animals brought in the *yajna* and offers sacrifices with his own hands. Therefore, instead of good deeds, he does inauspicious deeds." After the kind teachings of Lord Buddha, Prasenjit's heart transforms. He freed all the animals locked up in slaughterhouses for sacrifice in the *yagya* in the kingdom. The religious impulse was awakened in his mind at the very first contact with God. He thanked his queen Mallika for this virtuous benefit, but sometimes king Prasenjit, becoming more passionate about the security of his kingdom, started to deviate from the path of righteousness. Then Mallika explained to him, "O lord, to discipline the subjects and council, power, terror and the harsh rule is not needed, rather compassion and friendly behaviour is required. The whole kingdom was terrified by the terror of the dacoit Angulimal but as soon as he went to Lord Buddha, he too gave up all his weapons and became a worshiper." Prasenjit is a king but he is also a husband. Hearing so much praise of another man from the mouth of his wife, he got enraged, got angry, he himself reached Purva Rama monastery to test Lord Buddha. Where Bhante was giving discourses in the *Dharma Sabha*. Hundreds of audiences are present there, all are calm and disciplined, the *Shravak Parishad* is very polite without the use of any weapons. After witnessing this scene his heart changed completely. Due to the efforts of queen Mallika, devotion to Lord Buddha was awakened. Compassion towards the subjects and friendly nature towards the council of ministers led to peace and an environment of prosperity returned in the kingdom. Mallika started meditating while staying in the palace. When the king asked her, "Mallika, who do you like the most?" He has a hope in his heart that Mallika will take his name as her most loved one but he did not receive a wilful reply. Truthful and introspective Mallika has rightfully recognised the truth of *dharma*. On that day Tathagata announced this before his monk's sangh, "Queen Mallika is the foremost among the self-realized seekers".

❏

Utpalvarna

The birth of a girl child always creates a wonderful joy in the house. In the feudal era, everyone wishes for a male child. But the girl child is not placed before the rights of the son, yet the birth of a girl child is respected in the upper class and *varna* now when *maata* Lokeswari gave birth to a girl as a first child, everyone heartily welcomed her. Father is a commander. Full of chivalry and bravery. All his life he has fought for the side of the regional king. He does not like the harsh reality of war. But what can one do if he has been born in a *Kshatriya* clan and has done hereditary service in the army. The father's heart was overwhelmed at the sight of his tender daughter like a blooming lot us. Such a beautiful girl, such a clear skin complexion, he does not remember that he has seen such a beautiful girl in his lifetime. His wife Lokeshwari Devi is also a very beautiful woman, but the girl has definitely incarnated in the form of some of her divine ancestors with *Lavanya*. According to the rituals, the girl was named after three fortnights. He has direct contact with the royal family, which is why the king and queen themselves came to her naming ceremony. There is no girl as beautiful as her even in any royal family. After much study, she was given the name Utpalvarna. Anyway, the Lotus flower is not only considered a symbol of beauty but also a symbol of purity. Utpalvarna started to grow up in her father's house, amidst the service of caretakers. Just as musk is in the navel of a deer and its fragrance spreads all around on its own, similarly the fame of the form of Utpalvarna has spread all around. *Rajguru* himself comes to teach her literature, numerology and grammar. Being a beautiful woman sometimes is very harmful. But if the woman is very beautiful and with a sharp intellect and is *Lavanyavati*, then this confluence also becomes inauspicious for a father. Even the son of her maternal uncle, who in relation is the eldest brother, has also become blind to the beauty of his ancestral sister. He also tries unsuccessfully to get her. According to tradition, marriage between brothers and sisters who are closely related by blood is prohibited. In the feudal *Kshatriya* society, it is considered a heinous crime.

*Koli*ya dynasty, *Nag* dynasty, *Shakya* dynasty and *Rajputra* have started sending gifts to Utapalvarna at every festival. It is the wish of all *Kshatriya* dynasty royal families that their son gets married to a high *varna*, cultured, educated, decent and beautiful girl so that all those qualities are found in the off-springs and their descendants can attain the best caste, *varna* and they can in the world. All the princes were ready for war among themselves. Everyone wished *Varya* Utpalvarna. Father only wants to establish peace. He knows that his daughter is special. It seems impossible to find a suitable match. Utpalvarna's maid is like her friend. She tells her all the secrets of her mind. Utpalvarna is very much in love with her beauty. She also envisions a handsome prince. Requests her father to hold a *swayamvara*. She will only garland the one she thinks deserving. Swayamvara was held in the auspicious time of *Vasant Panchami*. *Kshatriya* dynasty princes and kings of all ages, adults and teenagers, were present and they displayed their strength. When the well-dressed Utpalvarna sees herself in the huge mirror, she becomes fascinated by herself. Maid Kushala weaves her long hair into a braid and weaves Jasmine flowers. Tall physique, glowing skin like a blooming lotus flower, *Mrignayani (Deer eyed)*, adorning the braid of long black hair like *Nagin* has been decorated with flowers and entering the swayamvara ceremony with a garland in her hand, all become speechless for a few moments. No one has seen *Apsaras* (Angels) in their lifetime, only heard of. The *Apsara* (Angel) of their imagination is present with a garland. Gradually, Utpalvarna moves forward with her maidservant, but none of the men matches the prince in her imagination. All of them are wearing silk clothes, wearing diamond and ruby rings in their hands, displaying their magnificence and valour by holding weapons in their senior arms. In everyone's eyes, only the image of sensuality and lust is visible. Like every man wants to consume her. The spirit of courtship does not spill out in anyone. Now, what will the logical, intellectual test do to them? Utpalvarna does not choose anyone. Father knows the consequence of this. All the present contestants were shocked. Such a daring girl, as if she walking away after thumping their existence. A man always desires dedication from a woman. If a woman rejects him, then his ego suffers. Then he can go to any extent of destruction for the satisfaction of his ego. All the princes present started preparing for war among themselves as if as soon as they fight, they will win Utpalvarna and take her to their kingdom. Inside the building her father was horrified as he knew of the dire consequences of the war. He requests his daughter to accept one of them and establish peace. But Utpalvarna is proudy, a man inferior to herself is not acceptable. She clearly said, "I will not accept any of these undeserving men, they are not worthy of me. Don't force me and if you give any other orders, I will gladly accept." The helpless, apprehensive, frightened father said in anger, so to keep the peace in this situation, you not getting married is appropriate. Any marriage can never be successful with the colour of bloodshed of innocent men. I command you; you give up the life of material opulence. It is heard that Mata Goutami has obtained permission from Buddhist monks to breed nuns. You go to their shelter." Angered by this proposal of her father, Utpalvarna immediately accepted it. The father sent a message through the messenger, the girl has decides to become a nun. Now she will not tie the knot with anyone. Now all the warriors are discouraged, it is inappropriate to accept her by force after she deciding to become a nun. Disappointed warriors again started marching towards their respective kingdoms with a heavy heart. Utpalvarna's decision created a wave of surprise in the entire state. None of the citizens wanted to witness such an extraordinary beauty become a nun. But the path of meditation is very tough. Utpalvarna is no longer interested in worldly luxuries. She took off all the ornaments on hers without the help of the maidservant and threw them away. Relinquishing the silk cloth worn on the body, she put on *Kasai*(cotton) clothes. Mother Lokeshwari cried seeing this condition of her beloved, but there is no effect of mother's tears on Utpalvarna. She has renounced these things in her mind. Giving up external things would have been as difficult as turning away from one's own physical beauty. As soon as she renounced everything, and started going to Maha Prajapati Goutami, then the maid Kushala said, "Goddess, you will have to cut your hair." Hearing this Utpalvarna's heart sank. How could she possibly renunciate her dense black hair, nails, bone marrow and blood, it is also an integral part of the human body. No, she will not shave off her head. Kushala explained that without shaving off the head she will not be able to become *upsampadika. It is a prerequisite to become a nun, or else* your resolve will remain incomplete. Utpalvarna started crying now, she renounced her hair weeping but kept a bunch of hair strands hidden in her box. She could not give up its fascination. After a long journey, she returned to Jaitavan and appeared outside the monastery of Goutami Mata. Mata Goutami made her aware of all the conduct and rules of joining the *Sangha*. She forgot all her anguish in front of the loving, compassionate Goutami. Tomorrow morning, she has to be present in front of Lord Buddha himself. She is to be initiated by him. Throughout the night Utpalvarna kept placing her hair strands from the box on her forehead and kept weeping. She is clinched by the cravings. How will she face *Bhante*? After taking a bath in the morning, Utpalvarna bowed down to Bhante and sat in the rearmost row. How should she look into the eyes of Lord Gautam who has attained Bodhi knowledge? Right now, she is full of cravings. How will *Bhante* give her initiation? *Bhante* smiled seeing her and said looking at her, girl, this body is mortal, don't fall in love with it, you have to sacrifice your craving on your own, I am only a guide, you have to walk on your path of spiritual practice. Utpalvarna saw that there is no one else in the auditorium, there is only *Tathagata* and herself, in presence of *Tathagata*, she saw an image of her dreadful appearance like dull skin, falling hair, insects eating bone marrow, unhealthy sick physiqueand she is so fascinated by her little hair. That image vanished in front of her eyes. *Tathagata* is sitting in a meditative posture as if there is a radiantly illuminated atmosphere all around. All the nuns who were praying started chanting *mantras*. As soon as Utpalvarna realized, all the cravings in her mind vanished. After bowing, she quietly left from there. Going to her room, she put the hair strands hidden in her box in the river flowing outside. Now there is no anger in her heart, there is no attraction for beauty and there is no greed for youth. She has sacrificed all the cravings of the mind. Now she is calm and fulfilled, she does not have any kind of scrape. She does not even remember the splendour of her father's house. Now she is a disciple of the *Sangh* and has gradually started taking charge of the operator. At that time nuns used to roam around the city and collect alms. Educated nuns used to spread the teachings of Buddha. In the onset of evening, outside the city, they used to stay alone by making their huts in the forests in the peripheral areas. Utpalvarna has also come along with other nuns to preach and spread to *Saket*. Everyone has made their own hut in the park outside the city. Arrangements have been made for sleeping by laying sackcloth on the ground itself. Wooden doors have been installed so that no wild animal can attack. The nuns do not take food at night. After travelling the whole day, providing education in meetings and eating whatever is received in alms, they stay in the hut only during the night to sleep. To give to the tired body, it is essential to sleep at night. In the night she recites *ShantiPaath*. They remain silent and do not communicate with each other, this is their simple routine. Some anti-social elements want to disturb these nuns during their migration, but they are not able to dare because they get protection from the king of the state. But there is no dearth of evil criminals in the society. That night Utpalvarna along with some nun's companions went to the city to give discourses, walking barefoot throughout the day and held meetings in many places. Discussed *Dharma* with the followers of Buddha. After having lunch at a disciple's place at noon, she got busy with her work again. In the evening, exhausted, she entered her hut. But she did not know that her uncle's wicked son Rupanand was already ambushed in her hut. Anand had learned from his aunt, Lokeshwari Devi, that Utpalvarna, being a nun, travels from city to city. She preaches *Dharma*. Anand was married, but he was not yet able to get rid of the entanglement of beauty in the form of his sister. He wanted to get her by any means possible. When a man fails to get the love of a woman, he wants to get her by force and one of the purposes of getting her is to have physical contact with her by force so that she will be compelled to accept him. The evil Anand searched for Utpalvarna for many months and only this morning he got information about her hut. Anyway, her hut is located outside the city near the forest, no one can come to protect her. Like a trickster, he hid in a corner of her hut and waited for Utpalvarna to return. Just as Utpalvarna entered the hut after the evening, the feeling of animalism awakened in Anand's mind, tired Utpalvarna in cotton clothes without her hair in the dim flame of the small lamp was shining like a lotus flower. The rag wrapped over her body is unable to cover her youth. Anand's sensuality reaches its climax as soon as she opens her thongs and sits in the posture of rest. Unable to control himself anymore, Utpalvarna extinguished the only burning lamp so that she could rest in the darkness. She is not afraid of the darkness, but as soon as she lies on her bed, Anand comes and grips her by force. Utpalvarna was completely ignorant of this type of attack, she could not understand at first who was using his physical force on her. She pushes him back in a hoarse voice and asks, "Who are you? Don't you feel ashamed to do such a despicable act? I'm a nun, get away from me, don't break my modesty, I'll punish you" – *Balishtha Rupananda* who used to call as Anand with love by the family members said - "Dear, don't you recognize me yet, how much I love you, your old lover. You come back with me into family life. Don't waste your youth and beauty by being a nun. I will give all the pleasures of the world." He kept on saying all this but did not move away from Utpalvarna even for a moment, rather it was as if the ghost of mental insanity mounted on him. Even after Utpalvarna's shouted and insulted him, he started having sex with her and raped her. He knows that a woman's modesty is her honour, if her modesty is breached, she will not be able to show her face to anyone due to shame and will dedicate herself forever and Anand will enjoy her beauty lifelong.

Hearing the shouts of Utpalvarna, the nun present in the nearby hut came running. Seeing such plight of her companion there, she was shocked. Anand has no remorse for his ill actions. He knows that society will only blame the woman, will call him a *patita* and he will be innocent and the winner of this misdeed for life. As soon as he stepped out of the hut the other nuns condemned him but no one attacked him because in their tradition they cannot kill anyone. Taking advantage of this situation, Anand started going towards the forest. But even nature does not forgive anyone for such a heinous crime. A few moments later a heart-wrenching cry was heard. Anand started mourning to save his life. No one knows whether Anand has sunk into the swamp or has fallen under a rock or some wild animal has killed and eaten him. Whatever happened after that night the body of Anand was not even found, nature immediately gave the fruits of his actions to him, but the nun's union is confused, what to do with the victim Utpalvarna, it is not her fault, but there has been sexual intercourse with the nun, worldly pleasures, sex, entertainment are prohibited in the union. The nuns took the news of this incident to the Tathagata. Maha Prajapati Goutami took care of Utpalvarna. Even if the crime was committed by her wicked cousin, the worldly blame fell on her. That's why a meeting of both the unions was called, the whole situation was described in front of *Bhante*. *Bhante* had apprehension in advance that such charges could be levelled against the nuns. He heard the full description from Utpalvarna and said that Utpalvarna is completely innocent in this. Guilty is the person who has committed this sin. Just like lotus flower blossoms in the mud, but remains blameless, like dew drops cannot last on flowers similarly, the blame of rape on a woman of character by an adulterous wicked cannot tarnish her womanhood. Bhante said that "Utpalvarna is a nun, she is a qualifier; worldly pleasures cannot stand on her. She has conquered even the craving. In that act of rape, she did not experience anything and did not accept anything. Just as the raindrops cannot stay on the petals of Lotus, they have to fall, just as the ripened earrings of wheat can never hold the grains tightly, they have to fall similarly, there will be no ill effect of this crime on the body of Utpalvarna. She is innocent. Utpalvarna is unblemished in a crime committed against her will, by force, deceit." This decision of *Bhante* was justified by everyone, Utpalvarna worked as the fore-manager of the *Sangh* for many years. Mata Goutami also felt that it is not their world to control anti-social evil forces. But for the protection of the nuns, she requested Lord Buddha to allow the establishment of a monastery for the nuns in the city and this resolution was passed. In Sankashya village, many nuns with Utpalvarna were permitted in the monastery of the *Sangha* and after that those nuns started residing in every *vihara* as a union. After the incident of Utpalvarna, this revolutionary decision was taken. There are eight rules of *"Ashtadhamma"* which are mandatory for every nun to follow.

First- Hundred-year-old sub-educated nun must also greet a *monk* who is of her rank or a *monk* of a lesser rank.

Second - If she violates the rule, she will never be able to become the best nun.

Third – During the monsoons, she will never go to a village or city where there is no monk and she will never stay alone.

Fourth - After every 15 days, she herself will ask the date of *upostas* and sermons of the Bhikshu Sangh and will follow the sermon accordingly.

Fifth - Visible hearing of the nun in front of both the *sanghas* after the end of the rainy season and the faults of the *parishakti* should be prevented.

Sixth - On committing serious wrong doing, the nun should plead before both the unions.

Seventh - *Shikshamana,* who has learned the *Shata Dharmas* in two years, should receive *upasampada*from both the *Sanghas.*

Eighth - No nun should under any circumstance speak abusive words towards any *monk* or give any sermon.

From time to time, the possibility of such accidents increases, as Shubhashvari had also thought it appropriate to remain blind by giving both her eyes and not to become the life partner of an evil adulterer.

At the age of 82, Utpalvarna attained Nirvana.

❏

Krishna Goutami

Keshugupta, a wealthy Seth lived in the city of Saket, he was very miserly. He used to give loans to poor people on interest. If they were unable to repay the loan on time, he would usurp his property. While doing this, he collected immense wealth, but unfortunately, his son was always sick, he was physically very weak. Once Seth went to another city for business. There he saw a beautiful, gentle and amiable teenage girl carrying flowers to the Devi temple. On her way back home, he saw that the teenager was distributing *prasad* to the leprosy patients sitting on the road. The sick and poor from the body are rejoicing after receiving *prasad* from that girl. Seeing their face, it seemed as if their sufferings were healed and new energy had been infused into their body. The girl was moving forward by touching with her hands while bowing lovingly to everyone. Seeing the gentleness, charity and beauty of that teenager, the idea of making her his daughter-in-law came to Seth's mind. Keshugupta had never done anyone any favour in his lifetime, he had never done any good to anyone by spending money on any kind of event in his house. Even he had never donated money or food to any poor person. Mesmerized by the behaviour of the teenager, Keshugupta inquired from the people present there and came to know that the girl's name is Krishna Goutami. He approached her father with a proposal of marriage for his son. Krishna Goutami was the seventh child of her father, who was loved by not only her parents but also other people but they were unable to get her married due to lack of money.

When the proposal of marriage of Krishna Goutami came, her parents started thinking that Keshugupta was a wealthy Seth and he had only one son. On getting married, their daughter will be the owner of all the property and enjoy the opulence. Krishna's parents did not want to spend money on organizing the marriage due to lack of money and Keshugupta wanted the same because of mental poverty. As decided by both the parties, as soon as *Chaturmas* was completed, Krishna got married to Keshugupta's son on the first date of *Muhurta*. As soon as the marriage took place, Krishna became the sole owner of her father-in-law's house. There was only one maidservant to take care of the household chores, but Krishna was very happy to be the mistress. Krishna was filled with the spirit of charity, religion and service, so sometimes she secretly gave alms to the poor. Her husband being a patient, never interrupted her in any work. The married life of both of them was passing happily for some years and after seven years she got the happiness of motherhood. She gave birth to a beautiful and healthy child. Here, as the age of Seth Keshugupta increased, he also got sick and died after a long illness. After the death of the father, Krishna's husband became very depressed and because of this he started to remain unwell.

Anyway, when a married woman becomes a mother, she becomes alienated from her husband to some extent. She devotes all her attention, energy and time to her beloved child even more than her life. Krishna did something similar. She knew that her husband was physically weak and would be incapable to give birth to another child. That is why Krishna Goutamishowered all her love and affection on her son. Within a week of the father-in-law's first death anniversary, her husband passed away. Everyone knows that whether the husband is healthy or unwell, cruel or kind, hardworking or vile, he is the biggest and most important support for a married woman. After becoming a widow, Krishna started living alone in a huge house with her only child and trusted maidservant. Anyway, according to tradition, entry of widowed women is prohibited in any auspicious work. Now she used to spend all her time on the upbringing of the son while staying at home.

When her beloved child spoke in his childish language, Krishna's heart would have been overwhelmed. She would forget all her pain. She would feed him with her own hands and make him sleep by singing sweet lullabies at night. She handed over all the household chores to her maidservant, even to the extent of not keeping an account of profit and loss. Her only asset was her child, but the wheel of time is always spinning and it never remains the same. When her son was three years old, she called a *Brahmin* and gave a pen in his hand, duly performed a *yajna* and started his education so that her child could become an educated man in future. After this event, her eyes saw thousands of dreams in the night. Her son has become an accomplished scholar. He has been selected for the post of General Secretary in the royal court. The girls of all the republics are eager to marry him and the vibrant lad who became the General Secretary obeys only his mother's orders. She was immersed all night in such unique dreams.

In the morning she got up and took a bath, then took her son to the well to take a bath. While there, the child started jumping while playing in the water with his mother and suddenly fell on the ground. By the time Krishna Goutami could understand anything, disaster had taken place. The only support of her life, dear to her more than her life, her son was lying in front of her in a dying state. After falling on the ground, he had gone into the lap of the goddess of death due to a deep stroke in his brain. Krishna lost her senses for a few moments. Not a single tear came out of her eyes and in a hurry, taking her son in her lap, ran madly towards the royal doctor. The Royal doctor was getting ready early in the morning and was leaving for the *Raj Bhavan*. Suddenly, seeing a small child clinging to her chest and seeing a semi-conscious widow coming towards him, he was surprised, *"Devi*, tell me what is the matter, do not panic so much." Krishna Goutami said, "My son has fainted, please cure him by giving medicine. "The experienced royal doctor said, "First put your child on the ground so that I can see, then only I will do the treatment." Krishna hastily placed the lifeless child in front of the royal doctor. The Royal doctor touched him and understood that he was dead but how to convey such a sad thing to his mother? He slowly explained to Krishna and said, *"Devi*, your son is no longer breathing. He has left all of us and gone to another world. No *sanjeevani* herb (medicinal herbs) on earth can cure it. Go, don't cry, he only has this much life. Be patient and cremate the child." Krishna was not ready to hear anything like this. Angry at the royal doctor, abusing him, she said with disgust, "What kind of royal doctor are you, if you do not have *Sanjeevani* herb and are unable to cure him, then do not lie. I will get my son treated by some other doctor." Royal doctor was understanding Krishna's mental state and therefore remained calm. By humbly folding his hands, he returned to his house with a heavy heart. Krishna kept running here and there, clutching her dead child to her chest. Even her maid kept on weeping and following her, but she failed to understand Krishna Goutami.

Krishna after visiting every house in the city distraughtly requested everyone to bring her *Sanjeevani* herbs so that her son's life could be saved. The housewives' eyes filled with tears after hearing her heartfelt cry, the men were also helpless, expressing sympathy for her deranged condition, but everyone was helpless in helping her. After the incident happened in the morning till evening, she kept crying in front of every house on every street of the city and kept on requesting. Disappointed from all sides, she started walking towards the forest. Seeing a calm, gentle, monk coming from the front, a ray of hope flashed again in her mind and she said, "O *Bhante*, give me the *Sanjeevani* herb, heal my son, bring him back."

The monk looked at Krishna calmly and said, "O *maate*, be patient, I will bring back your son's life with the *Sanjeevani* herb." On hearing this, the hungry, thirsty, tired Krishna got some mental relief. She said, "So don't delay and give life to him." The monk being in the same calm posture says, "*Maate*, don't be impatient, just bring me some mustard seeds as alms from some house, I will make *Sanjeevani* herb out of it and give it to your son." Clenching the child to her Krishna was about to run immediately towards the city, the monk said, "*Maate*, keep one thing in mind, mustard seeds will be acceptable only from those families who have never mourned any death in their house." Crazy Krishna said, "It's just such a small thing, *Bhante*, you just wait for me for a few moments, I will bring mustard seeds right away." She once again knocked on every gate of the city and started asking for some mustard seeds in alms but with that, she also started asking, "Has there ever been death bereavement in your family?" The house owner would take pity on her and say, "Go don't waste our time. Somebody has died in every house." Some have lost their mother, some have lost their father, someone has lost his brother and someone has lost his child, no house has been found where there have been no deaths. Disheartened Krishna again reached the monk outside the city, where it was now evening. Small lamps were twinkling all around the city. All the people after completing their routine were waiting to sleep after dinner. At the feet of the monk Krishna started crying clenching her child to her chest, bowing her head, the monk said, "*Maate*, this life is mortal, if there is birth then there is a death too. Man is tied to the cycle of life and death. Look at the city's lamps, some burn for a few moments, and some burn for a longer time, but by the last hour of the night, all are extinguished and there is sunrise again in the morning." Krishna slowly raised her head and looked at the monk. Then she looked towards the city. Some were completely extinguished and after some time the crest of all the lamps disappeared. All went to the lap of the sleep goddess. She started seeing those huge compassionate eyes of the monk. She came to learn about this harsh truth of life. Everything is mortal, then why and for whom so much attachment? Her deranged, depressed mind became completely calm. *Buddha* continued on his path and the consciousness of Krishna Goutami started following him. She conquered the grief of death.

❑

Visakha

There is a small village in Uruvela region - Rampura. A beautiful girl was born into an educated family there. Father teaches in *Gurukul*. The source of income is limited but they are very happy with the birth of a girl child in the house. His wife Sushila is also faithful. She runs her household with the limited income of her husband like a *sugrahani*. The qualities of both the parents are equally incarnated in the girl child. She is as intelligent as her father and patient and charitable like her mother. She has seen from childhood that her parents have no greed for money. Whenever the mother cooks in the kitchen, and anyone comes to her door for alms, she gives them food in charity with a free hand and also feeds them. Daughter Visakha is also very charitable. Whatever toys or precious clothes she has, she distributes them among the children of the poor. She even gives the fruits lying in her basket to the hungry poor. She knows that there will never be a shortage by giving charity. Nature definitely fulfills our needs. Once a monk came to her house early in the morning. As the food was still being cooked, Vishakha donated a pot filled with milk in her kitchen. The monk left satisfied giving infinite blessings. Due to this nature of hers, the villagers used to love the teacher's kind daughter Visakha very much. Just as the fragrance of a fragrant flower spreads on its own, it does not have to make any effort on its own, similarly, the wisdom, charity, and humble nature of Visakha are talked about far and wide. All families want their sons to have a daughter-in-law like Visakha.

Dhananjay is the richest *Seth* in Shravasti Nagar. The search is on for a suitable daughter-in-law for their only handsome son, Punnajay. *Seth* has also heard about Vishakha. According to the tradition, he sends a marriage proposal through the *pandit*. Mother Sushila is proud of the fate of her daughter. Vishakha gets married to Punnajay at an auspicious time. A cultured, intelligent, educated teenager from a small village is now the best daughter-in-law of a splendid city like Shravasti. There are slaves and maid-servants in the house, food stores, cowsheds, huge buildings etc. Vishakha, skilled in household work, has taken responsibility of the entire family smoothly. She takes special care of subordinate employees. She especially favours the agricultural workers. According to the needs of everyone, gives them their rights. Whenever a monk comes, she donates with a free hand. The husband says in a pampering manner - "Dear this way, my father's accumulated wealth will one day be exhausted." After hearing such a thing, Visakha's heart remains very sad. She thinks, "What is the use of so much wealth when it cannot help anyone in need or calamity? Doing charity purifies the wealth and the heart is also purified." If all the riches in the world keep on accumulating then how much inequality will be created in society? Who will take care of the needs of poor, hardworking, labours and monks? Who will be their support? After death, this wealth will not go with you. This wealth will not even go up till the crematorium. Then why is there so much attachment to this wealth? Such thoughts always agitate her but she is unable to convince the head of this house. Wealth will be exhausted, this charity of yours will surely give us a place in heaven after death, but in a living state we will become a pauper. Visakha knows that her husband is saying this in a gusto manner but the head of the family is her father-in-law. He does not like charity at all. He has also instructed his daughter-in-law in very strict words - "Don't give anything or food, money without my permission. All this is my accumulated wealth."Vishaka is a cultured daughter-in-law and she will never disobey the orders of her father-in-law who is equivalent to her father. Once when *Seth* Dhananjay was having his food in the afternoon, when the daughter-in-law was serving him that very moment a monk came at their door. He stood there with alms pot. Vishakha knows that if she does not give food to the monk today, he will remain hungry. *Seth* is eating a variety of delicacies on a silver plate which is placed on a wooden stool inside. Vishakha looked at her father-in-law, his eyes reflected a muted impression of disapproval. She does not want to annoy the old headman by arguing with him during the meal and knows that a housewife should not quarrel while serving food. If there is a quarrel during that time, then there will be a dearth in the family. Therefore, coming out and folding both hands to the monk in humility, she says humbly - "Sorry, there is not much food in the house today." The monk says - "Maata whatever food the family is eating give me some from that itself. In reply, Vishakha says - "The food that my father-in-law is eating is stale. How can I donate stale food to you?" The monks go ahead giving his blessings, but the daughter-in-law's words pierce *Seth's* heart like thorns. This girl is so daring, she tells the monk that I am consuming stale food even though I am having fresh food.

Such an insult to the heir of the Migar dynasty. He wants to punish his daughter-in-law for this crime. In Shravasti Nagar there is a *panchayat* of their *varna* society. He will take such a downgraded woman to the*panchayat* and teach her the harshest lesson of life. Thinking this, *Seth* went to the *panchayat* with his indictment. The next day, the *Panch* sat in front of the whole society, he sent a message to the daughter-in-law to be present. Her husband's mind stopped working out of fear. He is aware of his father's anger. He cannot see an innocent wife getting punished, but he also does not have the courage to stand against his father. Vishakha with utmost humility boldly appeared before the *Panchas*. The Panchas asked, "O *Devi*, have you really spoken such words, how can your father-in-law eat stale food?" Wise Vishakha saluted all the senior members of the society present and then simply said - "The food that my father like father-in-law is eating, he got it from the fruits of his past lives. He has done some such good deeds, due to which he is getting such nutritious, healthy and edible food without any effort in this birth, so he is using the fruits of his past *karma* in this birth. That's why this food became stale. That's why I told this to the monk." The *Panchayat* was satisfied after hearing this answer from the intelligent woman. They found Vishakha's answer justified and courteous. They did not accuse her of anything and respectfully allowed her to enter the house, but this answer of the daughter-in-law settled in a completely different way in *Seth's* mind. He came back home but started trying to know the meaning of the words of his daughter-in-law. It was as if his dormant consciousness had woken up, his conscience shook him. In all truthfulness, he did not do any hard work in this life, did not invest money in any good work, yet he is getting such tasty food. The privilege he has got of being *Seth* in this birth, he is destroying in his greed, lust and attachment. "Oh, what a terrible crime he is committing." Today, his daughter-in-law has removed the shadow of greed from his eyes. Just as a mother speaks bitter words to bring her lost child on the right path, similarly Vishakha also wants to make him realize the knowledge of the truth." Suddenly Migar *Seth* saw the image of his dead mother in his daughter-in-law. He started crying. He started accepting Vishakha as his mother. Made her the rightful owner of his immense wealth. Vishakha is happy now. She donates freely. The stories of her donation have spread far and wide. With the passage of time, she was blessed with a son.

Vishaka, grateful for *Tathagata's* kindness, tells her husband - "Go to Kunddhanvan and invite the *Bhikshu Sangha* and the Buddha for a week's meal." On the next morning, he reached Kunddhanvan. *Tathagata*, having completed his daily work, had taken a bath and was sitting alone outside his *Gandhkuti*. Worshiping him, he requested the *Tathagata* to accept food for seven days along with the *Bhikshu Sangha. Tathagata* remained silent. This is a sign of his acceptance. He immediately reached home and informed Vishakha about the acceptance of the invitation. She was very pleased. She knew that Buddha and his *Bhikshu Sangha* take food only once before noon. So she prepared a variety of dry, juicy dishes with full devotion and reverence. The Tathagata along with his monks arrived at their residence at the appointed time. The devout head of the house Migar Seth became very humble and devotional.Tathagata along with his monks reached the house of Migar Mata Visakha forenoon. After having food Visakha sat down on a mat and said, "*Bhante*, I ask God for eight boons." "Vishakhe, Tathagata has gone beyond blessings." "*Bhante*, I will only ask what is right and that is innocent." Then *Bhante*said - "Speak Vishakhe." Vishakha was very pleased after getting the permission of Lord Buddha, she asked for eight boons.

1 - I want to donate *chiver* to Yavat Jeevan Sangh.

2- I want to donate food to every monk who comes to Shravasti.

3- I want to give charity to all the monks who leave from Shravasti.

4- I want to cure sick monks.

5 - I want to donate food to the attendants who serve the sick monks.

6 - I want to donate medicine to sick monks.

7 - I want to give *Yavagu (khichdi)* to the Bhikshu Sangh every morning.

8 - I want to donate udak-sari (clothing) to the Bhikshuni Sangha to wear at the time of bath.

After listening to so many boons, God asked the reason for them and then Vishakha said - "Lord! *Dhamma* service leads to accumulation of merit." "But what will you get from this?" Vishakha, *Bhante*, Lord, my mind will be happy, with such love my mind will get pleased. By this I will experience happiness and my mind will attain *samadhi.*" Then *Bhante* said - It is true that by giving charity with a skilful mind, there is joy. Charity of *Dharma* conquers all donations, love for Dharma conquers all love. Destruction of craving conquers all sorrows. Vishakha with her child goes to Buddha's Gandhakutir to seek blessings. Throughout the day she remains present there in *Dhamma* discussions with nuns. A thought arises in her heart that, there should be a huge vihara for all of them, where they can discuss the *Dhamma*, devotees should be present in large numbers and get benefited from his words that are equivalent to blessings.Before evening, taking blessings from *Bhante*, carrying her son in her lap, she goes back to her residence. After her departure, the eyes of the *agrasevak* Anand fell on Vishakha's bundle. A large bundle wrapped in silk cloth. *Bhante* orders that Vishakha has forgotten it here give it to her abode at the earliest and come. The next morning, taking the bundle, they reached Vishakha's house. They politely want to return her belongings but Vishakha is not particularly excited to see her lost bundle. She says - I had forgotten this thing. This item is of no use in my life. What will I do with this? I had left it in the monastery, that's why you should take it back to the monastery." Anand said - "But how will it be possible." Migar Mata said affectionately - "This is my donation to the *Sangh*. Please present it at the feet of *Bhante* and use this donation amount for the work of the monastery. Anand returned with the bundle, he is very intelligent. He knows that Vishakha wants to donate indirectly. After reaching in front of *Bhante*, when he opened that bundle, all the monks were astonished. It was filled with jewels of priceless diamonds and rubies and gold coins. Vihar Sanghas do not accept gold ornaments. What will they do with these ornaments, on the other hand, Migar Mata has donated it to them. She won't even take it back. Everyone is in a dilemma when Anand, showing his practical intelligence, proposes that all these ornaments and gold coins can be sold to the goldsmith of the city and with the cash that they will get, a huge, excellent Buddha Vihara will be built. *Bhante* remains silent on this proposal which is his acceptance. Immediately the biggest goldsmith in the city was called. He too was astonished to see such valuable and rare jewellery. He valued them at several crores of rupees. A lot of money was received, by which special craftsmen and painters and artisans were called and a huge, beautiful, wonderful *vihara* was built. Independent houses (chambers) were built for all the nuns. A huge auditorium was established in the central part. A separate building was constructed for the worshipers coming from outside. A very beautiful *Gandhakutir* was built for the Lord. Vishakha became the first worshiper. Later, when a son was born to her son, after fulfilling all the duties of her family life, handing everything over to her son and daughter-in-law, she went to the *Sangha* with her husband. Seeing so much peace, ease and simplicity around there, her mind became blissful. Freed from family shackles, she started clapping loudly and chanting loudly - "Omshanti" "Omshanti" this voice echoed in the nunnery all around. Some nuns thought that she had lost her mental balance, but Buddha told them that she has achieved her goal while going on the path of ultimate peace, which is why she is so blissful.

The charity of Vishakha has also been praised by Lord Buddha himself – he has said "This woman lives in a worldly environment. She deserves the favour of kings and queens. Yet her heart is calm and steady. She is youthful and surrounded by wealth and opulence. Yet she remains unmoved and thoughtful in the path of her life, which is a rarity in this world." Even today worshipers and housewives consider Vishakha's charitable, discreet and considerate nature as ideal. *Sangha* has a special place in Buddhism. If anyone donates, firstly it goes to the *Sangha*. Monks make their living by only the food donated in the alm spot. Once when Gautama Buddha had come to Kapilastu, his mother Goutami was moved to see his *Kashaychiver* in winter. She weaved winter clothes for him with her own hands and took both the blankets and presented them to him. Then *Bhante* humbly requested her to give this donation to the *Sangha*. They will use it however they want. The Mother wants to cover her son's body with a cloth woven with her own hands, but Lord Buddha did not accept that as well, then Anand Sevak took both the blankets from the mother's hands and placed them in the Sangha and then requested the *Guru* to sit on one of the blankets. There should not be any attachment or affection at the time of giving charity. The *Guru* wanted to give this message to everyone. Migaar Mata Vishakha does not donate in the desire to get something or any attachment or illusion. She sees all the *monks* and the poor with equal eyes. She does not wish for any kind of blessings from them. This is the true form of charity.

❏

Chandalini

Nature has its own laws. Sun, moon, planets, constellations, sky, mountains, hills, rivers, springs, oceans, lakes, air, sunlight, shade and rain, she gives everything equally to all beings and does not discriminate between anyone. Animals, birds, aquatics, mammals, snakes, insects, moths and even molecules and bacteria she favours all equally. There is no discrimination in her power, there is no high and low. Mankind is the only being that wants to conquer nature. Wants to establish his dominion over it and in this greed and lust does many types of abominations which are against the law of nature and also destructive. Exploitation and hypocrisy are born from the definition of divinities that he creates based on invisible, unreachable, latent, imperceptible, untouchable etc. to prove himself supreme. The whole world was divided into small and big countries, the one who was capable, clever, cunning and opportunistic, only he would rule. By exploiting the subjects, doing war and sacrificing his soldiers and expanding his state territories. He establishes the religious system as per the fulfilment of his wishes. Presents himself as a divine power. Gradually, this system was based on the principle of divine legitimacy of the king and the principle of passing from father to son in the same lineage, the common people were fascinated by the state power and the divinity of the king. The helpless subjects used to be afraid of God and the invisible. The kings who considered themselves to be of a special caste, they were called *Kshatriyas*, people of the stature of *Rajguru, Raj-Jyotish* etc. were pathfinders for them, to the kings and feudal lords under their control, they used superstition, casteism to draft the preamble. In which no one can challenge the combined authority of King, Rajguru and God and the subjects surrender completely to them. That is why for centuries the fearful and affected people could never muster the courage to raise their voices against poverty and exploitation. The subjects were divided into different varnas, castes and classes where *Brahmins* and *Kshatriyas* were mounted on a higher pedestal. *Vaishyas* also used to run their business very smoothly in a wealthy state, now remain the last varna which is the backward class, the upper caste people would address by calling them a lesser caste. For years, he was surviving away from social consciousness and served the people of higher classes with impunity because the stem of society was not based on karma but birth. Keeping unwavering faith in this tradition, the oppressed class considered sorrow as their fate.

Champa Nagar is a small village on the banks of the Harinay River. On one side there is a flowing river and a small mountain range towards the north, nature has been a special blessing to this village. Despite the abundance of copper and iron deposits in the plains of Magadha Raj, the soil of this village is very fertile. Wheat, millet and paddy are cultivated. Rani's palace is only one and a half *Kosh* (Miles) away from the village. Many women of the village go there daily to render their service. *Malin, Thobin, Kaharin, Sairandri, Nahan* to adorn the queen, entry of all women is permissible in that palace in some form or the other. Not that they are respected like other upper-class women or get special facilities, but for their services, they get the company of women of *Brahmin*, *Kshatriya* and *Vaishya varna* family, but below all these, there is one more class left, they are named *Chandala*, they do only untouchable work. Cleaning of excreta and urine coming from the palace and city, cremation of dead bodies in the crematorium, all such major works which if they postpone even for a day, then all the palaces, cities, streets, highways will become contaminated, the whole atmosphere may be filled with a fierce unbearable odour. That is why in the social system, this *varna* considers this to be its fate and performs this task with impunity without any indictment. People call them wonderful. They do not allow even the shadow of their body to fall in their house, well, pond, rivers, temple and kitchen. Not only their entry but presence is also prohibited everywhere. Purity comes after their work is over, but they are impure. A coincidence of nature, a beautiful healthy girl has been born in Chammu Chandal of Champa city. Husband and wife are ecstatic. Kundalini after her marriage has been going to the crematorium with her husband for many years. Sometimes she picks up silk clothes draped over the bodies of dead people and brings them home because at the time of cremation there is a tradition of making the body undressed. At the time of the death of a rich person, sometimes the rings of a golden coil or ruby worn in his hand remain. Then the Chandal has the right over all of them. Kundalini has collected a lot of silk cloth clothes and some ornaments. Even the dreams of a poor, exploited, helpless mother for her future child are no less than the dreams of queens. She also looks at her daughter as the world's most beautiful girl. Whenever Kundalini goes with her husband to clean the dirt flowing in the drains, she does not take her daughter along. The girl's name is Prakriti. She only plays in the courtyard of the house. When she grew up, she sometimes went to bathe in the river, but as soon as she reached the ghat - "Chee: what are you doing here Chandal's daughter? run away from here, you have defiled us. Now we will have to wash all the clothes again and have to take a bath again." Hearing this, without understanding anything, she returned home very hurt and asked her mother - "What is this Chandal's daughter? What is this untouchable? What is impurity? Tell me, mother?" Kundalini kept quietly looking at her dear daughter with moist eyes. She says - "Look at that *Rani*, this old well outside the village, this is ours. Its water is also very sweet. You fill water from here and take a bath here." "But mother, I have to take a bath in the flowing river." The mother explained, "That river flows at a very fast pace, it comes from far away mountains, that is why it is much polluted. My dear daughter's skin will be affected. You take bath here."

The innocent Prakriti obeyed the mother, then spring came and a big fair was organized in the city. Many merchants brought different types of clothes and materials from abroad. Wearing the jewellery and silk clothes kept by her mother, she also went to that event, it was the first experience of roaming for the simple and innocent village girl, many beautiful men and women in gorgeous and attractive clothes were roaming around. The mind of the teenager Prakriti got excited. Truly the fair is vast and alluring. When a young man looked at her, she would be happy in her mind, but seeing her dress, many women were amazed because she was wearing such a precious silk cloth, a golden earring. No one ever seems to be adorned in the things demanded or begged, something similar is happening with her too. Suddenly the queen's special maidservant's eyes fell on her and she shouted, "Hey look at the guts of *Chandal's* daughter, now she will roam around the city with us, this *Chandalini* will pollute the whole event." All the girls ran away shunning her. The boys' loving sight now turned into hatred. Many even shrugged their nose and mouth in disgust. "Ah: what a painful torture." The young girl recognizes, the love, hatred or sensuality in the eyes of men in a moment. Such a gross humiliation, she felt that she was standing alone and naked in the midst of the whole society and everyone was looking at her strangely. As if their eyes are piercing her skin, striking her inner being. They are inflicting such a wound that even the coolness of the full moon will not be able to heal.

The sweet blowing wind of spring is burning her androgenic hair to ashes. The huge sky above her forehead is laughing at him. The strong paved path built on the ground beneath her feet is piercing her like thorns. She has no name here. There is no existence, she is untouchable and she is *Chandalini*. Shrinking in herself, saving herself from her horrific humiliation, drinking a sip of hatred, she comes to her holy hut like a defeated *Chandal's* darling daughter. Now she has calmed down. She does not insist upon anything with her mother. The mother sometimes goes to the crematorium during the night and offers prayers to some invisible deities, but she no longer has faith in the power of God. Father's caress, mother's affection and any season changing in the environment do not effect on the *Chandal* girl. Mother's mind understood everything, but she is helpless in this exploited, unjust social system. If only a Chandal son of their caste is found, then she will get that teenage girl married. The cycle of life is now going on cumbersomely. The mother would go out every day to do her work with her husband, and the sad, calm, humiliated, neglected daughter would do household chores only by staying at home. Some Buddhist monks of Sravasti have come to the city for discourses. They fill their stomach by asking for alms from one house to another. The women of the rich family especially invite them to their house and serve them food. They are considered special guests of the king's family. They went to have lunch at Sthvir Seth's place in Anand Nagar. Women served food with great devotion. The food was delicious. Anand was a little late in finishing the whole meal. He quickly washed his hands and face, took his alms bowl and started towards the monastery. In a hurry, he did not even drink water after the meal. The monastery of the monks was very far from the city, there was no arrangement of water anywhere on the way. If he goes back to the city, it will be night. The monks do not go to any house after sunset. Chanting the mantra, Anand started moving forward. Now his throat started drying due to thirst, only then he reached Champapuri. There he saw a girl drawing water from the well. Anand approached her and said, "Oh girl, give me water, I am thirsty, my throat is feeling dry. I am also a bit tired due to travelling long distances. Kindly give me some water." Saying this he presented his alms pot in front of her. The bewildered girl started looking at the handsome beggar. She had never seen a man in such a costume before. Shaved head, broad frontal, sharp features. A tall mighty monk, wearing a strong body tavern, the pupil of his eyes are very stable, calm sight, charming smile, fatigue, face slightly withered but there is no lack of radiant glow. Such a handsome man is praying to the *Chandala* girl for alms. She stood confused. Again, the monk said - "Give me water, I am thirsty." Suddenly as if the girl woke up from her sleep, she said - "O Bhante, I cannot give you water, go somewhere else and take water.

Forgive me, Bhante. I cannot commit this crime." The monk asked in amazement - "What crime? It is the first duty of a human being to offer drinking water to the priests." The girl looked at the monk with a sad look, shrieked a little, then calmly said - "Bhante, forgive me. You will incur sin by taking water from my hand. I do not want to be a part of this sin. I am a poor untouchable girl." If the shadow of the people of my *Chandal* caste also falls on someone, then that person becomes untouchable, then how can I give you water with my own hands." Anand now understood the whole situation, he laughed and said - "Innocent girl, I have asked for water, water quenches thirst. I have not asked you for your caste in alms. You and I all belong to the human race. We all have equal rights on justice, education, equality and freedom." The girl said but I am an untouchable. The monk said - "Humanity opens the paths of knowledge equally for all. I do not accept this social discrimination. Man is not evaluated on the basis of his birth but on the basis of his deeds. Your work is great. You remove impurity from society and make it healthy and touchable. You are the leader of the complete order of society. If you do not do your work, then this whole system will crumble and break. You are a symbol of purity, give me water." The words of the monk wash away all the scum, hatred, animosity and despair in her. Now as if true sense she is beginning to feel like a human. Immediately putting her earthen pot in the well, she starts drawing water with reverence and with great devotion and affection, she offers water to the monk. At that time, as if the cycle of time stopped, the form of the whole human race has become one. That supernatural and phenomenal moment changed the whole life of the *Chandal* girl. The monk being satisfied drank the water and then by blessing the girl proceeded on his way. The girl felt blessed. She realised that man should be her partner who gives respect to women, a woman surrenders to her. Now the image of that gentle idol monk has settled in the girl's mind. Now she only has one wish in some way she could get that monk. The whole day she remembers only that monk. Her mother saw how her dear daughter is getting mad. It is never appropriate to experience suffering.

Coincidently again a group of monks passed through Champapuri. The girl impatiently requested the monk - "Bhante, you consider all mankind equal, then eat today's food at my house." The monk has realized the thoughts of the young girl's inner mind, but he can't reject her offer because he has freed her from the inferiority complex of being untouchable. This time if he refuses her offer, she will think that he doesn't see her equally. The monk accepted the offer. The girl had made all the preparations at home. She had made delicious food and served it to the monk. After the meal, the asked the monk to sit on her bed so that she could convey the feelings of her love to him and offer herself completely to the monk. Anand remembered his Guru's words. A woman's love is intense, she can absurdly do anything in her love. Anand patiently asked the girl - "Who do you love?" The girl replied, to you. The monk said to my body. Look at my body with concentration- as if hypnotised, she started following the words of the monk with complete concentration and she began to see the handsome strong body of the monk. Anand said –there are innumerable veins under this beautiful white - soft skin and there are arteries in which pure and impure blood is flowing. Look at the streams of red and blue blood flowing in them, the coating of bone marrow beneath it, the skeleton of bones, the ugly organs inside the body, there is nothing beautiful there. A mortal body, how ugly and terrible it is. There is no knowledge of how much dirt is inside the body. The face that you fall in love with, saliva flows in it, the nose is also full of dirt, there is filth in the ears. Intestine is full of feces - urine. Every element of the body is mortal, untouchable, impure and momentary. Getting the body only is not life. To attain the truth of life, one has to go on the path of spiritual practice. Society has always given it neglect, humiliation, contempt, hatred, inequality and severe mental pain. Why should it stay in society? It will go to that society where it will find truth, love, faith, belongingness and salvation. The untouchable girl bowed to the monk and went on her way because knowledge and respect are the right of the entire human race.

Anand told all of these things to Prakriti and said that for the welfare of the people, one has to move away from the virtuous path of the caste system based on birth, *Shudras* and *Chandalas* have become very inferior due to this corrupt system which has been going on for centuries. They are carrying this inhuman system for generations. Today, he who is considered as a low caste also has every right to become worshipped by following the path of righteousness. At that time, it was believed that only Kshatriyas and Brahmins were worthy of respect in society, even if they were devoid of modesty and virtues, and unreasonable, *Shudras* and women are subject to a lot of disrespect. Even if they are full of modesty and virtue. Tathagata had to work hard to rectify this. His first experiment of social reform was *UpaliNaiPravajya*, the *Chandal* girl, who was forced to live an extremely degraded life in her society, where even her touch is forbidden for the upper castes, she renounces that society and takes refuge in the *Sangh*, where there is neither sorrow nor pain, where Brahmins and Kshatriyas will also receive education from her. ❑

Patchara

This incident is from the time of Buddha. Then the structure of the *varna* system and the caste system was very complex and rigid. Republics were kingdoms ruled by autocratic rulers. The governance system of these republics was run in the manner prescribed by the jurisprudence of Brahmanism. Due to the rise of the *Vaishya* class, they had a lot of wealth and they measured their wealth in the form of livestock and money. The rulers also started adopting oppressive systems to establish their dominance at this time. Slavery was also becoming more prevalent. The ordinary poor, the lowest class citizens felt that their freedom was decreasing and the reason for the increase in their sufferings was the people of the upper *varna* and caste in the society. The Brahmins were pious but believed in rituals. They used to preach that man should first fulfil his responsibilities while living in society and adopt a life of renunciation only after taking a break from social life, but the rules of social life were different and unequal for all castes. The marriage ritual was exclusively valid only among the people of the same caste. Marriage of other kinds (out of caste) or in other *varna* was not allowed. The women who did not follow these social norms, they and their entire families were socially outcasted, but the *Shramans* used to travel like monks in search of spiritual knowledge. They belonged to the Brahmin or Kshatriya caste, but instead of living the life of secluded ascetics, they lived together in the forests as a spiritual group (*Sangha*) and did not accept caste discrimination. Like the *Shramana* republics, they organized themselves into autonomous unions and took all decisions through assemblies. They did not accept the existence of any Supreme God like *Brahma* or any creator in any other form.

In the *Kshatriya* clans of royal families, girls had the right to choose the bridegroom according to their wishes through *swayamvara*. This right was not given in the *Brahmin* and *Vaishya* castes, but more freedom was available to the girls in the *Shudra* caste. She used to accept marriage proposals with a man of the caste of her own volition, but there were social restrictions on women and they were also sexually exploited. That is why people of almost all castes considered it appropriate to marry their daughters in adolescence. The strict rules of marriage rituals prevalent in the society, mismatched marriage, lack of coordination in the couple, ban on widow marriage, outcasted from the society due to even small characterless behaviour, in all these traditions women have no option. Her mind becomes deranged caught in the web of various tensions. Society shows hesitation to re-accept her in any form. Then the woman wanders from city to city in this insane state. Sometimes, they are sacrificed to the sensual selfishness of the evil-natured individuals of society. It is matter of curiosity for the children. That is why seeing a woman in such an insane state, half-naked, hungry-thirsty, lost her mental balance, on the road, they start clapping, make her run on the city road or sometimes even hit her with stones and injure her continuously and try to render joy in the tones of lamentation. Her torn rags, burning with hunger, her stomach clinging to her back, dry, foul-smelling hair, eyes sunken in sorrow and wrath, blood oozing from countless wounds on her open body, how she has become like a vampire. The boys are teasing her by calling her a torn incision. Unaware of her revealing shame, the poor woman starts running on the road outside the city, wiping the blood that seeps from her wounds. The sound of the children's applause, piercing her ears, is striking the chords of her brain. She is not understand anything, in a faraway monastery outside, monks are reciting *mantras*. She reaches there listening to the sound of *"Vinay Sutak"* recitation and, standing in the same semi-naked state for a few moments in front of *Bhante*, seeing him for a moment, falls unconscious. Monk Upali quickly rises from his place and covers her with his rag. Everyone's heart fills with compassion. Outside the city, children and some conscienceless city dwellers still reach the monastery by calling Patchara-Patchara, but now she is in the shelter of Lord Buddha, in the shelter of the *Sangha*, in the shelter of the *Dhamma* and is safe, having lost her mental balance, deranged Patchara is now lying unconscious on the ground covered in the monk's robe. She is breathing. A woman has an amazing ability to survive even in adverse conditions. She survives even in so much sorrow and pain. Patchara is alive. The nuns pick her up and take her to their room. They bathe her a bath. Applying a paste of medicine on the wounds of her body and giving her food to eat, Patchara's body looks a little better externally, but mentally she has no consciousness. She keeps staring in the void. The next morning, taking her back to the auditorium, Goutami Mata presents her. *Bhante* remains silent seeing her. When she looks at *Bhante's* calm face, her soul is overwhelmed with a peaceful feeling. She falls at the feet of the Lord and starts moaning loudly. *Bhante*lets her cry, then after some time affectionately puts his hand compassionately on her forehead, as the hands of the Lord touch her forehead, thousands of waves begin to reverberate in her brain. She forgets the bitterness of her physical pain. Patchara slowly starts remembering the forgotten memories. *Bhante's* hands are still on her forehead giving blessings as if by means of waves he is taking away all the sorrows, pains and anguish of Patchara. Every moment is a wonderful experience, a supernatural form,Patchara begins to remember her entire past.

A beautiful girl is born into a wealthy family of Saket Nagar. She is very lucky. After her birth, the financial condition of the family starts to improve. The parents bring up Patchara with great affection. After some years a younger brother is also born to her parents. Patchara has great affection for her brother. Patchara's parents are worried about the beauty of their daughter. According to tradition, she wants to get her married in adolescence to a suitable, same caste groom, because the teenage years are very uncertain and confusing, lest their daughter makes contact with any wrong man, therefore they have prohibited her from going out of the house or going out to forests or boat ride. This is the law of nature, when you keep someone captive, subjugated, under extreme discipline, then he can go to any level for his freedom, breaks the traditions and becomes rebellious. The same thing happened with Patchara, her discipline-loving parents kept her as a prisoner at home for the safety of their dearly beloved daughter. There is no dearth of anything for her at home. They never let her get involved in household work. Never took any measures for her education. The whole day enjoying luscious food, laziness and luxurious life. He made the body a prisoner of the house, but her consciousness, her mind would roam in the open sky even without wings. As a teenager, it is natural to be attracted to the opposite sex. That attraction is so complex and difficult that it becomes impossible for a teenage girl to turn away from it. She could not describe or discuss these thoughts arising in her mind with anyone. She has no friend with whom he can speak her mind, no teacher or loving family member guide. There are slaves and maidservants to do every work at home and in these weak moments, Patchara gives her heart to the slave son who helps her in the household work. He also comes to work in Seth's house with his parents. The handsome, healthy *dasputra* has just entered his puberty. Youth leaves its mark on everyone. Patchara likes that young man. The young man is also eager to do every work on the orders of such a beautiful mistress. Where once he hated his servile life, now he felt blessed in the company and love of his teenage mistress. The magnet-like attraction started increasing in both of them. Every moment they would find an opportunity for solitude so that they could spend more and more time with each other. One evening, Patchara cleverly hid the slave in her room. The resident of the house thought that all the slaves and maidservants have left after finishing their work. Patchara anyway eats food in her room. She remained in her room after that evening. The slave hid under her sleeping altar. In the night, both of them told the things of their respective hearts to each other. The conversation of the mind, the attraction of the body, the unrequited love of that teenage years. The two made contact with love. Now they have reached that stage where they found it impossible to survive without each other and then what happened was not supposed to happen.

Patchara ran away from home one night, renouncing her father's honour with her beloved. In social traditions, such marriage is called "Asura marriage" and people of upper caste and varna do not accept it, but consider it a disgusting act and punish the couple who do so. That's why the slave son along with Patchara went to another city, where no one could recognize them and they could settle their family with love. Residing in Swapnapuri, the couple started their married life. When Patchara came hiding from her father's house, she had also brought some jewellery along with her. For a few months, they both lived in love, but after some time, Patchara came face to face with reality. Her husband no longer goes anywhere to work, but Patchara had to do all the household chores. He used to hate the practice of slavery and therefore her husband used his inferiority complex to victimise his helpless wife. After marriage, he has become her master and he would keep his woman like a slave and exploit her. The hatred and fury in his heart grew against the upper society class, the vengeance of all of this he would take out by torturing Patchara. Grieved Patchara has no other way, she quietly takes all the atrocities of her husband. After all, she has chosen this life and Patchara gets pregnant in the bitter experience of married life. When the seed starts growing in her womb, the love of motherhood awakens in her mind. She starts remembering her mother. She requests her husband to take her to her father's residence. Her husband does not allow this. He knows that society will forgive the girl's mistake, but the maid's son will be punished by giving it the form of a crime. That's why he does not accept this offer. As the baby starts growing in the womb, Patchara's mind starts to worry about meeting her parents. She knows that her parents will take care of her during the difficult time of delivery, and will also adopt her, and according to tradition, a married girl does her first delivery in her mother's home. Since morning her husband has gone out in search of work. Patchara walks towards her father's town without meeting her husband. She says to the housewife living near her house, "Sister, I am going to my father's house, when my husband returns you must give this information to him." and taking some of her old clothes with a pregnancy of nine months, slowly walks on the road towards the city. The path is very difficult, with forests and rivers, everything will fall on the way. With sympathy, she goes ahead alone with the hope that some sailor will help her to cross the river. On the other hand, the husband gets information that Patchara has left on a journey to her father's house. His masculine ego gets hurt. He is his master; how can his wife go without his permission? If Patchara does not come back to him in future, then it will be the biggest defeat of his manhood, "He does not want to live in the form of a slave, what kind of a master he is who can not even maintain his wife. Everyone in the society will laugh at him." And thinking this, he too quickly sets out on the same path.

He reaches very soon near the slow-moving pregnant wife. Now both of them start moving forward together but Patchara's labour pain starts on the way. At the earliest, she goes to solitude near the forest and she gives birth to a boy with great pain. Only a woman can feel how painful it is during childbirth and how painful it is to give birth if there is no experienced midwife or woman with her. For some days she has to take rest in the forest there. It is not possible for this mother to go to the city far away with the newborn. She comes to her residence with her husband. Patchara is not a housewife but a consumable item in this house. The lustful husband does not show even the slightest mercy to his lactating wife. Forcefully maintains physical contact with her with constant spirit, as a result, very soon Patchara becomes pregnant for the second time. One baby is breastfed and the other is growing in the womb, in such a dire situation, she shows her inability to give birth alone this time. Requests her husband to drop her at her mother's house. Till the time Patchara was single and young she was a material of attraction for her husband. Now in such a state, he is not even able to exploit her, the fulfilment of his desire remains incomplete, and he too has started wanting to get rid of this bondage. That is why he gladly accepts the offer to leave his pregnant, first child with his lactating wife. They both set out on the road leading to the city. The husband deliberately wants to take her to the river through the inaccessible forests so that he can run away leaving his wife alone in the dense forests in the darkness of night. Clouds have also formed, there is every chance of rain. The wife starts having labour pains in the forest itself. Poor Patchara again gave birth to a small child, suffering the pain of delivery alone. The child is born after seven months of pregnancy. That's why physically he is very small, so small like a child of a bird. Meanwhile, her husband is nowhere to be seen. The thunder of clouds, the river flowing nearby, assuming a fierce form, there is no human race around, the helpless Patchara sets out to find her husband. Her eldest son, who has not yet learned to walk, crawls on his hands and knees, makes him sit near her bale and explains, "You don't move from here, I will come back after looking for your father. The naive child, in wonder and fear, watches the mother progressing with sluggish steps lifting a lump of flesh. He also wants to follow his mother, but the mother has made him sit after explaining, he is not able to understand whether he should follow the crying mother or sit here and wait for her. Patchara has just woken up after giving birth and is not able to walk properly. She is feeling fear for her husband. Suddenly lightning strikes and she sees that her husband is sleeping near the rock by the flowing river. She runs up to him and picks him up, but his body has turned blue, foam is coming out of his mouth, and his heart is not even pulsating. Seeing the death of her husband from a snakebite, she starts mourning by beating her chest on his dead body. When her husband was going to cross the river leaving her alone in labour, a snake bit him and he died there in agony. Near the dead body of her husband, she begins her roaring cry like the roar of clouds. As if she was asking God for the reason for her miseries. Then her eyes fall on the eagle flying above. Which is flying fast and reaching the rock on the bank of the river. As if Patchara has suddenly awakened from consciousness. She gets reminded of her newborn baby. She tries to reach the banks of the river with all the strength of her life. She tries unsuccessfully to remove the eagle by screaming, but the speed of the pregnant mother cannot be compared to the speed of the eagle that moves in the sky. The hawk, mistaking a small seven-month-old baby lying near the dead body as a lump of meat, kills it with its beak, clings to its claws and flies away for the food of its offspring. Can there be any other terrible pain or sorrow in the life of a mother? The semi-neurotic mother keeps on moaning there for several days. She does not even have the capacity to cremate the body of her husband. Shakuni and the vulture slowly start gathering after getting the smell of the dead body. Nature follows its own rules. It does not depend on any social conventions. The defeated, painfully sad Patchara has to give up that place. She does not have the courage to see her husband's dead body being scratched by vultures and shakunis. Hearing her lamentation, her only one-and-a-nine months -old son tries running towards his mother while falling often. The little boy is unable to know the way in the heavy rain. Hearing his mother's lament, he starts moving in the same direction, panicking. The river is also in full spate during the rainy season. It is flowing breaking its banks. Just a big wave takes that boy in his lap and slams it into the flow of water. Hearing the cries of the child, Patchara comes back running. His little, cute child is drifting while diving in the river. With all her strength, she jumps into the river but is unable to swim to reach her child. In front of her eyes, her son falls in the lap of the river. Patchara's tears get washed in the rainwater and flow away in the river and take away all her feelings, the power to think and understand everything. The lost Patchara sits on the bank and then in despair aimlessly she turns to the river, crosses it and goes to her place of birth. When a person is defeated in all the worlds, he wants to go to his place of birth in the remaining period. On reaching the city, when she is moving towards the path of her home, she sees her friends and family members coming from cremation ground wearing white clothes. Seeing such a condition of Patchara, no one is able to recognize her, they think that some poor woman is sadly asking for alms. They start moving forward by scolding her. One of the elders says, "Go ahead girl, we cannot give you anything in alms now. There is a death thread in our *gotra*. Look at that Seth's house, his daughter had left the house a few years ago with the slave appointed for domestic work and since then the whole family was in great grief. When there was heavy rain here last night, both parents and their teenage son died due to lightning. We have come this morning after cremating them in the crematorium." The old man, showing a little sympathy, said, "You look very sad but due to the death in the family, till the purification process is not over, our donation will not be accepted. You go and take alms from someone else." Hearing this news, Patchara, a semi-neurotic, completely lost her mental balance, directionless, rag-less, foodless and shameless, she started wandering here and there in the city. People would turn their faces in disgust wherever she went. Torn rags, milk pouring out of breasts, postpartum haemorrhage flowing between thighs, dry scattered hair, sunken eyes after crying, skeleton-like physique without food, moving like a human spirit. The children by saying abusive words and hitting her with stones would send her out of the city. She doesn't experience anything. She is just breathing like a dead soul in a living body. Why is she still alive, this mystery is also not known to anyone, Patchara herself does not realize that she is alive and only then do those mantras resonate in her ears. The voices of the chanting go through her ears into her heart. As if a moment of life has been touched in the dead consciousness, like a few drops of cold rain on the earth scorched by the sun, evaporates but do not quench the thirst of the earth and the particles of the earth get anxious for the drops of rain. Thirsty earth starts getting impatient, in the same way, those mantras make Patchara impatient and she enters the *bhikkhu Vihara* without thinking, completely ignorant of her condition, seeing Lord Buddha in front of her for a moment she falls unconscious and falls down. This morning, after seeing Bhante, she became peaceful. How wonderful does his loving touch filled with blessings, like all the troubles of the body along with the mind vanished. Buddha is silent but Patchara is now in his refuge from his conscience. She has become a monk. She quietly follows all the rules of the *Sangha* and remains absorbed in the work with a sense of service. She no longer regrets any decision in her life. She has accepted all her guilt and wrong decisions. The terrible punishment she has received in life is also acceptable without any attachment or aversion. She no longer feels sad over all the events of the past, nor does she have any aspirations of any kind in the future. The craving is completely gone. She does not talk to anyone in the *Sangha*. She does all the work only with modesty. Due to her complete devotion, she is the most beloved nun of the *Sangha*. Once the meeting was over, when Bhante and his other disciples went to their respective rooms, all the nuns went out to take food and then she silently started cleaning the hall. She stands nearby a lamp placed there. On the first day when she had the darshan of the monk Buddha, the same light was coming from his face as well. She was then surrounded by a shadow of sorrow, but as soon as she came in front of Bhante, the shadow of pain, sorrow etc. had vanished. How patiently God had listened to all the events of her life and explained to her in very simple language that human life is mortal. Whoever takes birth, his death is inevitable. In this cycle of life and death, everyone suffers for their karma. Some live a moment like her younger son, some few months like her eldest son. Some have a long life like her parents and some dies in adolescence like their younger brother and some live only a few years like her husband. Everyone completes the duration of their cycle on their own. Everyone can share happiness, but he has to bear the sorrow, disease, pain and agony of his share. Bhante had given her the knowledge, "You are weeping for such little troubles, look around, human society is wandering in darkness from time immemorial, searching for the cause of its sorrows but does not try to find the remedy for that cause." That day

Patchara's troubled, sorrowful mind found stability. Now she would go ahead to redress the sorrows of women, of the sorrowful mothers who had come to the Sangha, because of the experience of the sufferings that she had experienced in her life. She would listen compassionately and patiently to their life stories and showed them the path of truth, by staying in the Sangha, she came to know that for self-purification, for pure thoughts of wisdom, one has to follow the path of continuous spiritual practice, only after studying the *Dhamma* with full devotion, we can use it in our lives. And now Patchara is very dear to the devotees. The way the *Bhikshu Sangha* is conducted by the beloved disciple of *Bhante*, "Upali", in the same way, Patchara started serving as the front operator of the *Bhikshunni Sangh*.

❑

Manvika Chincha

Rampura is a small village at a distance of two and a half *kos* near the city of Shravasti. It is the good fortune of the townspeople that theylisten to the discourses of Tathagata Buddha. Whenever Sakya Muni stays in Shravasti, not only the townspeople but also the people living in small villages far away come to the city on foot and get the pleasure of hearing the discourses from the Lord Buddha himself. They give donations to the Sangha. The monks make their living on alms anyway. They have never accumulated anything, nor do they have the greed of more charity and alms. The followers of humanity see everyone equally, that's why they are very popular. Man is very apprehensive about his future and that is why he does good and bad deeds to make his future strong and golden. The hypocritical guru never wants to share his power and ability with anyone. He keeps the innocent devotees in his false illusion. Sometimes they want to keep their followers tied in the *chakravyuh* of unseen forces, sometimes miracles or sometimes the law of the wheel of fortune and the *yagya* etc., but when they feel that their followers are now turning away from them and listening to the voice of Buddha. When those devotees are adopting Budha's teachings in their lifestyle, the *gurus* start feeling insecure. Tathagata's brother Devadatta hatched a conspiracy for the past several days and also got him attacked by the wicked, he made various efforts to kill Shakyamuni but he failed.

Now the speech of Gautam Buddha has become so much publicized that ordinary townspeople, rich, poor and even the feudal lords of the state started adopting the teachings given by him in their lives because the teachings of Lord Buddha are very simple and well planned. There is no *karma-kand, yagya-kand,* worship, caste-discrimination, religion-discrimination or class-discrimination anywhere in them. The same teachings for all are the way to a very elegant spiritual practice, like a person leading a weary, burdened life finds cool shade after the scorching sun. Gautam Buddha had eight simple principles - do not steal, do not misbehave, do not speak falsehood, do not condemn others, do not blame others, do not make an impure speech, do not covet, do not hate anyone, avoid ignorance and no pretence. It is a little difficult to follow these teachings in daily life but not impossible. Gradually, the teaching of the monk began to be loved all around. People's reverence and devotion towards him also started getting stronger and the same thing would knock his enemies. Enemie's future seemed bleak to them. They began to feel as if the people were turning away from the illusion of false religion laid by them and were getting attracted towards the monk. Some were feudatories, some orthodox Brahmins, some religious material merchants, and some were the relatives of the monk's family. Everyone had their selfish interests, but this time the enemy started thinking of weaving an idea of such a terrible conspiracy that they could destroy the monk and his disciples altogether. After much deliberation, the trick of the oldest period was played.

It is said that if the character of a person is publicly attacked with proof, then the downfall of that person is certain and the role of woman is very important in this type of evil process. Women are the cause of man's downfall and society, which does not see women with equal and high vision, blindly believes the stigmas imposed by women. Now the search for a woman started for this work. Although there is no dearth of town brides and devadasis in the city, the people had little faith in them. It was considered that women of an elite family, upper class and upper caste would be suitable for this karma. The search for such a woman was started in the city by their spies and after many days of tireless work, the Maha Mahant got information that there is a very beautiful girl named Manvika in Swapnapuri village in the east direction of Pava. She is from a noble family but is somewhat greedy by nature. The man she wanted to marry settled in another republic for business. Unsuccessful love made her even tougher. Now she pretends to love men but does not fall into anyone's love trap. She started hating the male caste in a way. By trapping them in the illusion of her beauty, betraying the love in their heart and taking gifts of their wealth, she would leave them tormented like a bird without wings. She has become adept at trapping false love and her speciality is that no one suspects her. She is so adept at misconduct, adultery, lying that till date she has neither appeared in this disguise in front of anyone nor was caught. On this information, the detectives were sent to her with a message. Special arrangements were made to call her to Sravasti. When she reached Shravasti sitting in a palanquin, she was fascinated by the natural beauty there. Enemies also arranged a house for her to stay in. She was told to go and accuse the monk of defamation of character.

Manvika accepted this deal because she was going to get a very attractive amount and now, she too was tired of false propaganda every day, she decided in her mind that she would go back to her city again with this amount and will marry her old friend Matrugupta. The clever Manvika immediately accepted the offer, but she said that it is not so easy and simple, it will at least take time of seven months. The enemies had no other option. They had to succeed in this conspiracy with patience and they knew that in the past all their attempts were against them. This conversation was kept completely secret. Manvika was now a resident of the city as well as started interacting with other housewives there. She was very skilled in the art of wooing people by talking sweetly. Gradually the people of the society accepted her. When the householders went to hear the discourse of the monk, they would also request her to "also come along". Manvika accompanied them for the discourse a couple of times. Whenever Bhante would be travelling to other republics for discourses then she would meet the disciples of Bhante and would come after listening to the philosophy and teachings of the teachers. Time was running out for her because she had to complete her work as soon as possible. In the evenings she would get ready and would walk towards Jaitwan from the city road. If a friend or neighbour would ask - "Where are you going in the evening" then she would proudly say, "I am going to visit and serve Bhante in JaitwanVihar. He has specially appointed me for his service." And this way as soon as evening falls, she visits JaitvanVihar and return to her abode only at dawn. In the night, she would rest in a separate building and on each *Ekadashi*, she would prepare the strategy ahead with the enemy. The rainy season has now started which will last from the full moon of the month of *Ashadha* till the full moon of the month of Ashwin. At that time the routes of movement in the republics were not smooth, safe and well-organized. The passengers were able to reach their destination only by battling their dangers. In the rainy season, sometimes the unpaved roads disappeared. Water logging and other natural calamities made the journeys more painful. Due to the fast water flow, the rivers also took a formidable form. That is why the travellers were compelled to stay in one place. After attaining Buddhahood, Tathagata Buddha resolved to take *Dharma* to the people for the welfare of mankind. For the propagation of Dharma, he used to travel from one place to another on foot along with his great *bhikkhus*. In this way, he would have direct contact with the public community. All the monks travelled barefoot. To avoid the natural and other calamities of the rainy season, Tathagata Buddha along with the *bhikkhus* would fulfill the resolution of his *Varshavas* by staying in a safe place, and engaging in meditation and study of Dharma. They also gained enlightenment from the Buddha's company and his sincere *"Dhamma Desana"*. Nearby worshipers and devotees gathered at that place to receive regular sermons from him and their queries were also resolved by the *Bhikshu Sangha*. During the day he would go somewhere for caretaking but rest in the monastery during the night. It has also become a tradition to fulfill the resolution of *Varshavas*. On the "Pravanaotsav" all the worshipers and devotees would donate food and clothes with gaiety, the *Bhikshu Sangh* wished for everyone's happiness and gives blessings while leaving that monastery and moving forward. During the rainy season, Manvika would pretend to go to the Jaitwan so that the devotees would trust her that she is spending the night there. Just like the flickering rays of the moon she kept wandering here and there so the townspeople started calling her Chincha. It has been three months since she has come to this city and now the beautiful *Chaturmas* has started. All the monks will stay here till the rainy season. All the devotees will offer daily so the enemy and Chincha started waiting patiently. Chincha, clad in splendid clothes, is now looking a little tired. She also limited the ornaments adorned on her body, which made her look a little duller. As soon as the *Chatumas* was completed, the townspeople celebrated *"Pravanatvas"* with great enthusiasm on *Ashwin Purnima*, it seemed as if the ocean of people had sprung up. The atmosphere around became very beautiful. Everyone was seeking blessings from Bhante. The donation of food and clothes for the day is now over. The next morning the Buddha along with all the monks will leave this Jaitavan Vihara. Not only the whole city, but the republic has also become the follower of Buddha. At the same time, Chincha entered the crowded meeting. She looks like a completely different woman. The bony young beautiful girl appeared in front of everyone as a pregnant woman. Her abdomen is protruding after taking the form of pregnancy of seven months. She is trying her best to hide it. She stood in front of everyone, covering her womb with her clothes. All the women looked at Chincha in amazement. Worshipers and followers also suddenly got confused by seeing her in such a form because Chincha is unmarried and "unmarried motherhood" is not respectable in society. Everyone kept looking at her shockingly.

.... One silent question in everyone's eyes is, "Who is the father? In the end, a worshiper asks, "Chicha, who has done this condition of yours?" Who is the father of the child in your womb? tell us. We will surely give you justice.

Will get you married to him. "Chincha first shrugged, then rolled her eyes down. When other women and townspeople started asking her again and again, she said in a very low voice, "Bhante is responsible for this condition." Due to this word, it was as if there was a thunderstorm in the assembly. The *Bhikshu sangh* was completely astonished, as all the followers were unable to understand anything and the hour of great confusion came. Many women had seen Chincha going to Jaitvan in the night but no one thought that the things heard would be revealed to them in this form today. This is unimaginable for all the human beings present in the meeting. Some enemies were also present in the meeting. They stood up and said - "O Goddess, don't you worry Chincha, we will definitely give you justice. If this disguised, pretender can betray you by taking the form of a monk, then he can do it to all of us. These *bhikkhus sangha* people will definitely get the punishment for this misdeed. We will all take them to the king. He will punish them and Tathagata will have to accept you. The person who calls himself the possessor of *Bodhigyan* has done such a despicable act, it is an unpardonable crime. Now the atmosphere of the meeting has become completely polluted. The assembly was divided into two parts. Some say that Chincha's allegations are true, while the other say it is false. When the intellect stops working, then work should be done with discretion, but in a crowd system, intelligence and discretion both does not work. The bhikkhus disciples got angry but they could not even attack Chincha nor could they say any abusive words. With a helpless look, Tathagata sat in a very calm posture as if nothing had happened. He is *Sthitapragyana*, he is not affected by happiness, sorrow, worry, joy or lamentation. He is Buddha. He opened his compassionate eyes and looked directly at Chincha's face.

For the first time today, Chincha had such a clear vision of the *Bhikkhu* Buddha.

..... His radiant face, coiled hair and compassionate eyes, what a great man he is. There is not even a trace of sorrow on the face, no ego, no anger, no restlessness. Immense stability just like *Sthitapragyana*." She is putting a stigma on such a great man. Who has incarnated on this earth for the welfare of mankind. Till date, no man has looked at her with such defeatist eyes and I am making such a terrible character slander. Then a disciple said, "She is characterless, a liar, mischievous and misdemeanour. By committing adultery with someone else, she is blaming that pregnancy on our *bhante*." The baby is still in the womb, as soon as it comes to the earth, it will be proof that it belongs to whom? But there is no embryo in Chincha's womb, to whom will she give birth? What will it prove? She started trembling with guilt, remorse, fear and misfortune. Worshipers also started remembering their gods O Lord, save us. Chincha felt as if the whole universe was spinning in front of her. Her parents, brothers, friends, lovers, conspirators and subjects are all disappearing. Only the calm face of Buddha is visible to her. The earth on which she is standing she felt a shiver. The trembling legs became weak and began to falter. One by one the old rags tied on her abdomen fell on the ground with her. She became unconscious and in an instant the secret of her pregnancy was revealed to everyone. Truth is like a drop of oil. No matter how big the water of the false may be, the truth comes to the surface like a drop of oil. Now all the rags have fallen on the earth. Chincha is lying nearby in the state of subconscious, not only her body but her soul also had a downfall. She dares to look at Buddha with a sense of guilt. The sound of *"chee: chee"* disdain reverberates from all around in the crowd, when she spins her eyes, she finds only hatred, ridicule, contempt and neglect in everyone's eyes. How can she survive with so much contempt? She looks at Buddha, pleading for mercy. When a man prays for forgiveness after committing a crime, when he starts burning in the fire of repentance from within, then there is no justification for punishing him. She wants to give up everything and take refuge in Buddha. It seems that her heartbreaking cry will tear apart the cool clouds of the month of *Ashwin*. Slowly all the followers started going towards their abode after taking blessings from Lord Tathagata. The people on the enemy side also started returning like defeated players towards their destination, stealing and hiding from everyone. All the *bhikkhus* of the *Bhikshu Sangha*, looking at Chincha in hatred with their heads bowed down on the ground, started going inside the monastery. Sun is about to set. Everything has become still in the golden red sky. Birds are hiding in their nests. As if everyone has found their destination. Buddha slowly rises from his seat and stands before Chincha. Chincha raises her head in shame and guilt and sees *Bhante* for the last time. With folded hands, the tears rolling from her eyes she prays for forgiveness. Due to grief, no words come out of her mouth. Intermittent hiccups expressing her sorrow. She starts rolling at the feet of Buddha, crying like mad. With both your hands she starts hitting her face very hard. Where will she go with this face? Buddha is silent which means he has granted her forgiveness but how will she spend this cursed life, where will she go? Buddha does not answer her. He turns his face in the opposite direction and goes inside their monastery. The full moon is shining in the sky. The sweet cool wind is all around. The flowers of tuberose and juhi have started blooming. Nature is so beautiful and calm. Chincha realizes from her conscience that nature is her mother. The land on which she was born will give her salvation. By going into the lap of nature, she will get freedom from this sinful life. Now Chincha's tears have stopped. All her sins were washed away by burning in the fire of repentance. She is coming out of *Van Vihara*, her footsteps are moving slowly in the lap of nature.

Chincha was not the only woman who made false allegations against Lord Buddha, another noble Brahmin girl was "Magandhi". She too was very impressed to see the beautiful and impressive face of Tathagata. With his extremely attractive physique, radiant face, huge graceful eyes, arched eyebrows, long nose, slender pink lips, lion-like chin and magnanimous bountiful forehead, she was so fascinated that she only wanted to have him as a husband. How many requests were made to him, her father also requested that "You live alone in the forest, if you accept Magandhi in the form of your wife, then she will serve you in the forest-migration." Then the *Samyaka* Buddha, with great patience and humility, replied to Magandhi's father - "Brahmin! I cannot take your daughter's hand. I have given up household life, I am *Geetaka*. I attained enlightenment sitting under the Bodhi tree." Now I am an *Arhat*, '*Samyak* Buddha', '*Sugat*' who walks on the right path. Not even the three beautiful daughters of Mardev, Trishna, Rati and Ragani could make me fall from *sadhana* samadhi. Human beauty has no meaning to me. I am free from all desires." Hearing this word, the Brahmin couple agreed and they followed the Buddha, but their arrogant beautiful daughter felt insulted and married King Udayan and kept on conspiring only after marriage. Sometimes against the queen Shyamavati and sometimes against *samayak* Buddha and the Sangha. Maharaj Udayan was a very dear devotee of Lord Buddha. Magandhi's false conspiracies caused her a catastrophe and the Maharaja punished her harshly. Buddha has said the true words - There is no fire equal to the indulgence of anger, no defecation like hatred, and there is no sorrow like five *skandhas* (beauty, pain, name, *sanskar* and science), there is no greater happiness than peace.

❑

Khujjuttra

The most dreadful of all the institutions that have existed in human society is the practice of slavery. The rich kings and the rulers who won the war used to enslave all the poor, underprivileged and exploited people. Not that everyone used to treat them cruelly, but the slaves and maids did not have any special respect from the royal family and the noble residences of the wealthy class. The slaves used to live their whole lives by bowing down and all they would get is food, clothes etc. only to live. They cannot become the owner of any property, land or money. Entry to worship houses and religious meetings are prohibited. The irony of their fate is simply living a life devoid of passion, lack of knowledge, senseless and sad. The maids are also often appointed for the personal service of the queen or the supreme bride and those maidservants, always keeping a sense of service in their mind, spend their whole life in their service. Kaushambi city is situated on the banks of river Yamuna and is the capital of Vatsa country. King Udayan considers Lord Buddha as his religious scholar. Udayana is the son of the*Chandravansh* and *shahastranik* king, a lover of literature and appreciator of art. He is amorous by nature. Although he has many queens, his love for Vasavadatta is more. Due to this other queens feel neglected. Another favourite queen of King Udayan is Shyamavati. Her family has old connections with Mathura. She is a lover of nature and after marriage, she had to come to Kaushambi city, leaving behind her gardens, and friends. Well, there is no comparison to the grandeur of Kaushambi. It is an exquisite city full of beautiful, huge atlases. Queen Shyamavati resides in her separate royal palace with her maids. There Dhaye who was declared the best in the city had a daughter Uttara. Dhaye has abandoned her since birth. The birth of a girl child in the family of maidservants is considered auspicious because in old age the maidservants feed their parents without any dilemma, but Uttara's fate is playing a different game. A flaw in the body of a very simple-looking girl has been found. She is hunchbacked, due to which she walks with a slight bend and to some extent looks ugly to normal people. No boy or girl meets Uttara, nor do they call her in any kind of game. Anyway, there is a religious belief among the people of civilized society that the person who has some disability in the body is incomplete, he is called handicapped and not disabled. People call them with distasteful and ugly words, treating them as laughable objects and insulting them. Uttara is a girl, above that a maid and that too hunchbacked as if the universe has sent her mercilessly to the earth. The townspeople and all the members of Seth's house called her Kubji, Kubju, Fujjuttara etc. and thus the most famous name came to be Khujjuttara. In Khujjuttra's life, there is no excitement, no wave, only humiliation, grief and pain. No one speaks to her even two words of love or sympathy. She keeps talking to herself in private. Repeats everything said to her very clearly, her speech has become such as the voice of a learned woman, but no one is affected by her voice because no one listens to her. Queen Shyamavati needs a reliable maidservant for herself, as soon as she gets the news, she announces from the city that she buys Dhaye's only neglected daughter as a maidservant. Khujjuttra now comes to the palace of Shyamavati and starts serving her. She finds her new mistress extremely compassionate and kind. Shyamavati is very much in love with flowers. She adorns herself by wearing a flower braid, garland of flowers and ornaments of flowers every day. The art lover King Udayan finds the queen's floral dress very enticing. Khujjuttra goes to the gardens every day and plucks many flowers and buys some of them, then makes different types of jewellery and makes the queen wear them. She embodies the ugliness and dryness of her life in the beauty and juices of flowers, she beautifies her afflictions and embellishes the queen. Shyamavati takes pity on her because of this beautiful art of her. In a way, she has charmed the queen. Now she lives near the queen. The queen talks to her respectfully. The beauty, decoration and the makeup of the queen, everything rests on the ornaments of flowers made by Khujjuttra. Taking four coins daily from the queen, she would go to the city to buy flowers, pick some flowers from the garden, buy some from the gardener and keep the rest of the currency with her. In a way, this is theft, but the maid Khujjuttra does not find anything bad in it. This cycle continued for many years.

King Udayana is the ultimate follower of Lord Buddha. He often comes and stays with his *bhikkhus sangha* in Kaushambi. Nagar Seth Ghoshit has built a grand maha*vihara* in a huge garden for his residence in the south-eastern corner of the city, so that whenever the Lord comes to Kaushambi, he can stay there, his *Mahavihara* is called Vishakata Ram Vihar. One day, after circumambulating a small hill outside the city Lord Buddha began to give sermons to the bhikkhus, sitting on a seat in front of the

Gandhakutir of Rama Mahavihara. "Monks! Do not do any such work with body and speech, which disturbs the happiness and peace of others. Never kill, don't steal, don't use drugs, don't tell lies, don't commit adultery and misery does not leave the wrongdoer. Therefore, we should not commit any sinful act, either secretly or revealingly." At that time, Khujjuttra was passing from there to collect flowers for her queen. She suddenly stopped at the gate of Ram MahaVihar. She heard the sweet words of Tathagata for the first time. On hearing the Buddha's words, the serene *Dharma* vision in her inner conscience awakened. She immediately came to know about the four noble truths (sorrow, the cause of sorrow, the cessation of sorrow and the path to cessation of suffering), and felt ashamed of her wrong actions. Immediately after buying flowers of all the currencies, she reached the queen. She no longer wants to commit unrighteousness with the earnings of sinful deeds. Queen Shyamavati is astonished to see so many flowers. She asks, "Uttara, how did you buy so many flowers?" Then Uttara without hesitation narrates the unreasonable act done by her i.e., theft. Accepts her guilt and apologizes. Queen Shyamavati is very kind and intelligent, she wants to know the reason behind this change in the nature of Uttara. Then Uttara narrates the whole incident in front of the queen and says, "For the happiness of many people, for the meaning, interest, happiness of the gods and human beings, having all these qualities is Tathagata, I have never seen any other sage, nor do I see it in the present apart from Tathagata. He purifies the mind and shows the path of freedom from sorrows." Uttara narrates the words of Tathagata with her clear, beautiful, truthful voice. The queen was very impressed to hear such words. The queen says to Uttara, "Oh, how much happiness, how much peace, how much coolness is there. I too have started experiencing the truth. Good luck Uttara, daily recite the *amrit* words of Lord Tathagata to me."

Now Uttara would go to Ram *mahavihar* every day and listen to the *amrit* from the mouth of the *Bhante* and then come to the palace and recite the *amrit* words in front of all the women and the queen. She was no longer the maid of the palace. The queen freed her from slavery. Arranged a dignified high seat for her and she along with other royal palace inmates, would sit on the ground in front of Uttara and listen with reverence to the voice of the *Bhagwan* Tathagata. Just as colour washes over a black-free white cloth completely and fully, in the same way the effect of the teachings of the Lord washed over the pure mind of Uttara very quickly and completely. Her life completely changed. While listening to the words of the Lord, she realized that all things that are born, they all perish and everything is mortal. She became a listener by understanding the impermanent religion and by accepting it from the innermost heart itself at the very first time. She was counted among the prominent householder disciples of Lord Buddha. Firstly, one should engage himself in an ideal way of life and then preach to someone else. In the same way, Uttara applied all the teachings of Buddha in her life and then preached. Due to Uttara's religious contact, Queen Shyamavati also shines like the star of *Shukra* in the last hours of the night, in the same way, her friendship started shining over all the virtuous deeds. The queen also got liberation of mind and because of her virtues she also became a leader in *"MaitriViharPraptKarni"*. Lord Buddha has said, "Khujjuttara is the foremost among many listeners" who first disciplined herself and then showed Queen Shyamavati the path of righteousness". ❏

Datta

The king of the Koliya dynasty has announced the *swayamvara* of his only daughter. In those times princes from different republics used to come to participate in the *swayamvar*. In order to strengthen mutual relations in different states, the kings used to get their children married to each other. Since the people of most of the republics were Kshatriyas, therefore the selection of suitable bride and groom according to caste, *varna* and class was done in a simple way. Although the system of eight types of marriages was prevalent, but *Gandharva, Asura, Pratiloma, Anuloma* marriage etc. were not seen with much respect. Goutami and King Shuddhodhana sent their eldest son to *swayamvar*, their eldest son is very adept in archery and science and is a master of sharp intellect. He knows that he is capable of winning the most beautiful princess in the world. His beloved younger brother also walks with the eldest brother.

According to the rule of *swayamvara*, no two sons of the same parent can participate in the *swayamvara* simultaneously. This tradition is made to keep away family discord or competition. Nanda is not here to participate in the *swayamvara* anyway. His age is less than 20 years. Men below the age of 25 years cannot enter the *Grihastha*

Ashram. Nanda is a symbol of *soumyamurti*, but war never pleases him. His soul is very joyful. The natural beauty, songs and music attract him very much. His mother knows that her youngest son is a bit lazy too. He does not remain immersed in pleasures, but the inclination of the mind is in that direction. Mother is also satisfied with this quality of his. She wants her son to be around her. Because the nature and conduct of the eldest son has kept her worried. There is sometimes a shadow of a feeling of detachment in it. Mother's mind is always apprehensive that her youngest Nanda may also be estranged from worldly splendour like his elder brother. That is why Nanda's attachment is very pleasing to her. When Nanda saw his elder brother defeating all the great experienced warriors in *swayamvar*, he went and embraced him with gusto and said, "I consider you my role model. You are so mighty; I want to become a warrior like you in my life. The hesitant princess Gopa felt blessed to have her dear, very handsome, intelligent, courageous husband as groom, she started bowing to her *Ishta Deva* in her heart. The eldest brother has to go back to Kapilvastu with his new bride but Nanda has yet to travel further. He said, "You leave for Kapilavastu with your soldiers and wife. I will go to my uncle's kingdom. Nanda along with his soldiers started towards Devdah. The maternal grandfather's house has always been dear to the grandchildren. He roamed day and night in the beautiful valleys of nature and went boating. Sometimes he even went on hunting. Once when he was boating, he saw some teenage girls doing water sports on the *ghat*. Young Nanda without blinking started staring at those water fairies. One of them, the smallest, slender white-coloured teenager, seems to be the most playful. She does not even care about her clothes in water sports. She is just deeply enjoying the water. The rays of the sun started shining like a diamond on her face. Suddenly, everyone's eyes fell on Nanda enthroned in the boat and all the playful girls started laughing except the young girl who compressed herself due to shyness. In a panic, she forgot to wrap her northern garment around her. Only by bowing her two eyes, she stood still, in the morning, in the cool water of the river, in front of Nanda with her beautiful skinny body, half-naked among her friends. That was the first love at first sight as if the beauty of all nature had been poured out on her by God. Although Nand has seen many young girls, but for the first time he saw such a naive, aliphatic physique. It's like he will fall madly in love with her. At that moment, both of them exchanged love and affection with their eyes without talking to each other. All the girls started going back to their abode from the *ghat*, smiling. The teenager also had to go with them, but her heart has become a prisoner to the young man on the boat. Nand also returned to the *Raj Bhavan*. His mind is nowhere. Impatiently he only wants to see the teenager again. Had he been in his own kingdom Kapilvastu, it would have been a different matter, where he would have traced that girl through his spies, but here he is a guest. From whom does he seek help? He could not sleep the whole night. The next morning, he rowed the boat, crossed the river and reached the same *ghat*, but there was no one there. The sad Nanda waited till the evening, then when the servants arrived from the *Raj Bhavan* looking for him, the defeated, silently followed them towards the *Raj Bhavan*. As the days passed, the girl had a place in his heart, he started crying remembering her. Seeing this condition of his, *Raj Vaidya* was informed. The experienced royal doctor gave the medicine, but in a slow gesture, told the queen that it could be a disease of love. Get him married soon.

Royal astrology was called. After calculating according to the date of birth, he said that there is no time for marriage yet, but this horoscope has signs of marriage. It was decided that after three months, when the time for marriage is there, Kshatrani Rajkanya would be married to him and then only he will be sent to Kapilvastu. On the other hand, the constellations of the astrologer's daughter are also doing similar moves. Father is very worried for his daughter Datta. He wants to marry her to a well-educated, cultured Brahmin, Datta is about to be a *varya*. A Suitable candidate is yet to be found. In front of the fate of his daughter, all his knowledge of astrology is useless and unproven. Datta has become detached lying down in her home. She is unable to concentrate on any work. In the evening, she becomes sad. After the evening the entry of girls into the gardens is prohibited, but her mind started getting so disturbed that without informing her mother, she went for a walk in the garden quietly. Thirteenth lunar day of *Shukla Paksha*, everything has become bright. The flowers of *Harsingar* are about to bloom, through their fragrance they are giving the message of their blossoming. At the same time, under the Champa tree, a figure was seen sitting unmoved.

Datta has heard from her mother that invisible souls roam around in the night and in fear she started screaming and started running in the opposite direction. That figure too, hearing the cries of a woman, started running after that woman in fear of some danger. She felt that someone had been bitten, as soon as he placed his hand on her withers, Datta fainted and fell to the ground in fear. The young man immediately caught her by her arms and saved her from falling and was surprised to see her face. His heart rate increased. The half-conscious girl in his arms was the same girl with water sports, Datta now slowly opened her eyes, finding herself in the arms of her dream man, she fainted again with joy. Now the time has brought Datta and Nand together. Datta recovers after a few moments but Nanda keeps her in his arms. He is afraid that she might go away again. Datta is also in adolescence and the touch of man is creating waves in her body and consciousness. She also makes no effort to free herself from the shackles of love. Both wish to be with each other, but Datta does not want sex in maidenhood as it is a sin. Her desire and lust are not under her control but her conscience is still awake. Nanda's courtship request is accepted by her, but when the impatient Nanda, who is in the bondage of social extremes, wants to get her madly in love, Datta proposes to marry him, but how will it be possible in this night ?

It is known from the conversation that Nanda is a prince of the Kshatriya dynasty and Datta is a brahmin girl. There are still three months left in the auspicious time of marriage. Waiting so long is not possible for both of them. They decide that they will surrender themselves only after tying the knot according to the Gandharva marriage. By weaving a garland of Champa flowers, under the vines of Harsingar, the moon of *Trayodashi* of Shukla Paksha, twinkling stars and constellations, considering all the trees and vines present in the garden as witnesses, both of them choose each other and start their married life. Royal astrologer is helpless now. The girl accepted the prince in *Gandharva* marriage. Physical contact has also been made. Now he cannot oppose this marriage in any way. They do not accept the fact that the girl has entered a lower caste than herself through *Anulom* marriage, but *Gandharva* marriage cannot be unacceptable either. There is no opposition to this proposal in the royal family. Goutami and Shuddhodana warmly welcomed their daughter-in-law. Nand is in comfort with his wife Datta. The circumambulation of Datta's rites begins only with Nanda and ends at Nanda. She has nothing to do with the joys and sorrows of the external world, with the sufferings of human beings. Then the news comes that the monk can no longer reside in the royal palace. He camped with his disciples in a vihara in the Upkul region. He sent his forward servant to call Nanda. Nanda is very attached to his eldest brother and as soon as he gets the information, reaches Vihar to meet him. Sees Tathagata having his food. Nanda bows down to him. Tathagata says, "Nand bring some salt, there is no salt in the food. Whatever we get in alms, we take it." Nand goes and takes salt from Anand and gives it to his brother. Brother does not allow any kind of emotion to be published on his face, but he is completely ignorant of his brother. He has tied his hair and made a bun on his forehead. No ornaments, no fleshy arms like the Kshatriya kings. Wearing only yellow rags on the body and no ornaments but how attractive and radiant he looks even as this unique monk. Sakya Muni said, "Nanda you are very intelligent, your mind is also very pure, society needs you for human welfare. Come with me, do spiritual practice, understand the secret of life." Nand was speechless on hearing such an offer. He cannot leave his mother and *Pranpriya* wife to become a bhikkhu but refusing his dear brother's first request is also not accepted in his mind. So, he returns to the palace after taking permission from them. Mata Goutami is very sad to hear that her dearest younger son has been asked in alms by the bhikkhus. But it is probably not acceptable to Datta. She angrily tells her husband, "What truth is attained by walking away from worldly affairs, renouncing the household? Kings are kings. He can bring a daughter of any varna, gotra, but here the bride is a brahmin, whether the gopa will accept it or not. Immediately message was sent to Kapilvastu. The reply also came very soon as expected. It is acceptable to Gopa. According to the complete rituals, Datta's farewell took place. It took a full month to reach Kapilvastu. In this one month Nanda did not stay away from his newly married teenage wife for a single moment. He would take full care of her at every place on the way. Stayed near her in the night. What more could young Datta wish for? She enjoys every moment of her first love, her first man and the company of her husband. Datta was given a grand welcome in the palace. Goutami Mata found Datta very beautiful. Her mannerisms have fascinated Goutami. Mata Goutami is now, rest assured for her very dear son. Nanda will never be able to go anywhere freeing himself from Datta's love.

Later, Nanda's eldest brother abandoned his virtuous, beautiful wife and newborn child and went in search of truth. The whole kingdom was in mourning, the pain of Yashodhara's mind, the separation Datta has experienced. Datta has seen that noble woman, like a *tapaswini*, taking care of her children alone. A lot has changed over the years. Nature is changing, but love for Datta in Nanda's heart is like that first sight of love. Dutta is sometimes proud of her husband's love. Sometimes she also feels shame in front of her maids. Mata Goutami remains very disappointed after Siddhartha's departure. She requests Nanda to take over the kingdom, " the monk who deprives a thief, a young adult, a sage, a king's servant, a woman, a maid and a sick person from his sangha, will he get the knowledge of the truth?" No, I don't agree with this. You will not go anywhere. Nand is also in dilemma. He is unwilling to go from within but he doesn't want to disobey the orders of his elder brother. He tells Datta "Please allow me to take refuge in him for a few days, dear. I will be back soon. I do not have the capacity to obtain divine power etc. by penance. My brother himself will return me to the material world. Datta's mind is very disturbed. She cannot live without her husband for a moment. She is not an ascetic like Yashodhara. She agreed to go before her husband's eldest brother against tradition, but Nanda and Goutami stopped her from doing so. Datta gave up food. Did not even take water. Opening her hair, she started moaning loudly like a defeated woman. Hearing her cry, even the birds of the garden were frightened and flew here and there. There was an atmosphere of instability all around. According to the stipulated time, Nanda had to go on the path of spiritual practice with the monks. He saw his oppressed wife Datta before leaving. His dry hair and gleaming face, filled Datta in his arms and said, "Dear, I will be back very soon, don't do this to yourself, I will be in trouble, no paths can separate us from each other. We are two bodies, one soul." Desperate Datta, full of melancholy, raised her eyelids and looked at her beloved, unaware of how many moments have passed but Datta did not blink, she wants to hide her beloved in her eyes as if he was leaving with an unblemished feeling. The maid Sushila and mother Goutami with great pain took Datta away from Nanda. Now all the tears in Datta's eyes have dried up. She has become stone-hearted, neither she speaks nor hears anything. Just keeps staring at Nanda leaving with an emotionless face.

Nand also went to the *Vihara* and was very disturbed. He shaved his head. He renounced the royal robes and put on the garb of the monks. Waking up in the morning, he would study the words of Buddha. Then he used to cry in the forest during the day. He made a woman-like figure of Datta by coating it with lime on a huge rock. The coal was rubbed into the shape of her thick black hair. By grinding the catechu, he painted her lips, and by bringing a rag of a woman from somewhere he dressed her and made the form of a living Dutta. Now every day for hours he would sit in front of that picture and lament. This news reached Lord Buddha through other monks but the Lord did not get disturbed. One day he reached Nanda. He took his hand in his hand and said, "O dear Nanda, come along with me and travel to heaven today". Nand felt as if his bulky body has become weightless. He is crossing the cold air, cluster of clouds and roaming around the universe. Countless constellations, stars and planets are revolving around them on their respective axis. Crossing all of it, both of them reached heaven. It is so peaceful there and so much slender, indescribable beauty, so beautiful which he had never imagined, Apsaras are dancing and swinging in the garden. She laughs as if pearls are flowing. Bhante said, "If you do penance with sincerity, you will attain enlightenment. All these Apsaras will be under you, you will be their master." In the longing to get the beauty of Apsaras, Nanda also forgot his beloved married woman. He promised Lord Buddha that he would prove it by becoming a monk with full devotion. Both returned from heaven to earth again. Now Nanda does not go near that picture in the jungles. Follows strict union rules. He has put his full consciousness in the path of spiritual practice. The knowledge which the forward servant Ananda could not attain even after serving so many years, he attained the divine knowledge, he went to Buddha for permission to preach and spread, so Gautam Buddha asked - "Angels (*Apsaraye*) are now yours. You kept your word". Nand said, "Bhante, I have no craving for anyone now. I do not have any kind of longing; you have guided me. Donated divine knowledge to me". Bhante said, "No knowledge can be donated to anyone. You have achieved it through your own penance and perseverance. There are no such Apsaras in heaven. That I had created an illusion, but now you have become free from the illusionary web of truth and falsehood. You are divine power." Nanda has now attained full *Bodhisattva*. All the people worship him with great respect and honour. The divine visionary Nanda followed and kept preaching the teachings of the Buddhist Sangha until he attained great nirvana.

This news has also reached the palace. Later on, the royal maids themselves, Vimala, city brides, politicians, wicked, cruel, bandit *Angulimal*, daughter of *shudravarna*, sometimes abandoned by husband, maid-child Gamini, Patchara, Vidushini, Rohini, Maitriya, whose modesty was tried to be violated, who were very beautiful, unmarried, euphoric, countless exploits, unhappy women entered the bhikkhus sangha, but Datta lived in solitude in the separation of her husband, sacrificing all worldly, material pleasures, giving up all worldly, material pleasures, the man who forgot her in the greed of attaining apsaras, now there is no place in her heart for that dear husband. When he had left her alone years ago on the orders of his eldest brother, that was his last meet. Datta did not do penance in the hope of any heaven, did not do penance by roaming in the forest, nothing is permanent in life, everything is fleeting, she has found this truth in her solitary life. Her name will not be written in any history, but in Buddhism, *Anamika Tapaswini* Datta will be alive in silence. Because she has no fear, no longing for no one, no jealousy, no love, no death, no fear and no God, some bits of selfless time is often meaningless. She no longer remembers that loving time of her life. The anguish of the bitter pain of her husband's separation has incarnated in the moral force. The unexplained mysteries in her heart, the unrequited love, the constellation of unconscious thoughts, which have been freed from elusive forms of completeness, concentration and dignity of their self. She finally got the first realization. Ever since human civilization has developed since time immemorial, since then only the householder *ashram* has been considered the best. The attainment of heaven or salvation for women would have been possible only if they followed all the rules of the householder's *ashram* without any opposition, this belief was prevalent. Women have been denied many rites due to many practical reasons. His entire field of work was only household life, neither becoming a *sanyasi* nor entering any ashram as a*sadhvi*. Datta has become free even by being tied to the strings of household life.

❏

Sanghamitra

There is a very picturesque village near Pataliputra, the capital of the small republic of Magadha state. The people here are peace-loving. The name of this village is Champapuri. There, an indescribable beauty is born in the house of a poor farmer. That girl is so beautiful that there is no other girl beautiful like her in nearby villages. Poor farmer has no source of income. The landless farmer prays to Mother Earth, that the goddess of the earth will be pleased and shower wealth on him. But this beautiful girl was born to him. With great hope, his wife named her first daughter, Subhadrangi, who had a very beautiful graceful physique. As she grew older, her appearance and beauty began to shine like the sun and dazzled the eyes of everyone. A solution strikes his father. He took his daughter to the emperor's court and in exchange for some money, he left her there.

Due to the beauty of Subhadrangi, now the maids and courtesans of the king's court started feeling jealous and forced her to do lowly work. The beautiful girl of the poor, who came in the gift, knows that in her situation this is her job. The poor have no choice or preferences of their own. She attained proficiency by doing things like massaging the body with her head bowed, applying body scrub, bathing, washing, grooming hair, etc. Once the king returned tired from the war, he said to his charioteer, "My body is getting very tired, make some arrangements for service." The charioteer saw Subhadrangi in front, he appointed her. The maidservant also served the king with perfect skill. The king was pleased and wanted to give her a prize. This was the only occasion where the maid could change her fate.

She made a humble request, "Your Majesty, I am an abigail. My father was poor in the village, but I am from upper caste. If you bless me with a child, I will be blessed." It is said that a man is always defeated in front of beauty. The servant now became the king's aspiration. When she got a son, all her sorrows and sufferings ended. The son was named Ashok. She became the chief queen of the king with her service and beauty and gave birth to a second son. The first son became very ambitious like his mother and a great warrior like his father. Their attachment to the expansion of the kingdom and to rule over the whole world also made him cruel.

He has also had to live in exile with his mother in a very painful situation due to the conspiracy going on between the queens and their children in the royal court. He does not believe anyone he became an emperor after his brothers and sisters were killed. A *Chakravarti* emperor like him who is a skilled diplomat and a cruel, efficient ruler was never there before him in his lineage. Mother was a follower of the *Ajivak* religion. The son also kept his faith in the same religion, but as he went on to win the war, he would feel an emptiness from within. All the kingdoms he attacks, he ruthlessly makes them accept his tales. In many treaties, he would marry princesses and keep them under him. But Maharani Devi is very calm by nature. No matter how many women her husband brings after marriage, she understands her importance.

The king is preparing for war on the big kingdom Kalinga. Maharani Devi introduces him to Buddhist monks with utmost ease and patience. At that time the queen herself is pregnant. The effect of Buddhism starts falling on the child in her womb. Some change is also seen in Ashoka's nature. He begins to respect Buddhist monks. But who can avert *Mahakal*? War ensues, and thousands of Kalinga warriors are killed. The emperor gets sad seeing the massacre and destruction all around. On the other hand, Maharani Devi gives birth to a beautiful, calm girl, just by looking at her face the emperor forgets all his sorrows. As if she is not a girl but a messenger of peace.

The emperor now becomes a complete follower of Buddhism, and starts working on the propagation of religion along with the Kaurvaki whom he had won and brought from Kalinga. By taking refuge in the Buddhist *Sangha*, they get immense peace and their first child daughter, a messenger of peace, grows up in the teachings of the *Sangh* along with her parents.

Seeing her affection and reverence, the king named her Sanghamitra. Later she had many more sisters and brothers, but Sanghamitra remained the most beloved child of her father. After taking birth in Ujjayini, the mother takes her to all the shrines of Buddha. She visited all the religious places like Shravasti, Lumbini, Ramapura, Pava, Sarnath etc. in her childhood, but still, she used to get impatient in her mind. She also wanders in search of Buddhist knowledge, all the teachings and philosophies of Buddha heard in the womb felt as if have been absorbed in her body. Participating in discussions with different religious scholars, she would see different rituals of worship and sacrifice, but her mind was not attracted towards any. She has seen and heard many stories of her father's cruel form. The father's mind has changed, but Sanghamitra's mind has always been inclined towards the teachings of the monks. Still, she could not find the goal of her life. She also shares her sorrow with her brother Mahindra, but no one has the answer. The king also senses the vision engaged in the mysterious search hidden in the calm nature of his dear princess. He consults his ministers on how to keep Sanghamitra happy and blissful. Poor worldly *pundits* and scholars will advise the girl! they said - "Your Majesty, get the princess married. When the women get tangled in the duties of the household, husband's love, children, etc., then, one will get happiness only in the trap of love of loved ones". The emperor and the queen found this proposal appropriate. As soon as Sanghamitra completed the thirteenth year, in the first auspicious *muhurta* she was married to the handsome prince Agrabrahma. The princess is now married. Her husband loves her very much. Everyone respects her in the palace. She goes with her husband to see the Bodhi tree. Seeing that huge peepal tree, she feels that the journey of her life will be completed only in the presence of this holy tree. How Lord Buddha must have attained enlightenment here? One by one the scenes started rotating in front of her eyes. The branches, the swaying leaves, the giant stem and the roots submerged in the earth, all have "Bodhisattva" in them. This sacred tree was touched by the Lord, he bowed here by touching the ground with his hand. Each particle here is a symbol of "Samyak Buddha". It is in the air of this tree that he used to breathe his life. She remembered the Buddha's teachings she received during her childhood when the time of great nirvana was approaching. In appreciation of Tathagata's prayers, fragrant flowers and sandalwood powder were showered. Then Shasta told Ananda, that the monks or nuns who strongly walk on the path of *Dharma*, are actual prayers, and by these supreme prayers, the Tathagata is satisfied, *gurukrit*, respected, worshipped and honoured, it should be done. That is why Ananda live from your soul.

What is *Dharma*? Modesty is *Dharma*, *Samadhi* is *Dharma*, *Praja* is *Dharma*. *Dharma* is to follow the path of modesty, *samadhi* and *praja*. One who is fully awake, one whose craving, animosity and envy all are gone, who is completely free, whose struggles and doubts are over, who sees the blossoming of a flower in the same way as the birth of a child and falling of a leaf in the same way as the death of his parents, who sees the beautiful and the ugly alike, whose compassion is equal for all living beings and non-living. The path of Lord Buddha is the one to end all differences. The philosophy of Buddha rests only on realisation. There, remembering all this, Sanghamitra had a realisation. She remembered how a monk had come to the palace and explained the Buddha's "Kalam Sutta". In it, the Buddha said that do not believe anything because it is written in a holy book, nor believe it because many people believe it, neither because some guru is preaching it, nor because Buddha himself is saying it, but examine yourself, experience it and believe it only when it is relevant for yourself and the world. Buddha says "You take refuge in yourself, not someone else's." Immediately Sanghamitra was freed from all her illusions and doubts, and she had to devote her everlasting life to the propagation of Dharma. Standing in front of the Bodhi tree as if her life became bright. She came back to the palace, but her heart, mind, conscience and feelings are only pulling her towards *Dharma*. Sanghamitra conceived at a very young age and gave birth to a beautiful, healthy child in due course. No motherly love, husband's love could bind her in emotional entanglement. She had lost her husband's support, but Sanghamitra is no longer distracted in any way. Her father sent his messengers around the country and abroad so that Buddhism could be propagated in all the countries. He sent his son Mahindra to Sinhaladweep. Mother Sanghamitra gladly sent her only son along with her maternal uncle on such a difficult and long pilgrimage without any delay. Staying in the state, she started taking charge of all the work of propagating the religion of her father. Now she does not live like a princess, she leads a very simple life. Being the apple of her father's eye, she would do all the work by staying in front of her father.

The Chakravarti emperor began to use the money of his kingdom freely for the propagation of Buddhism. Thousands of stupas were built. Inscriptions, *viharas*, sculptures and masterpieces of art were made. Sanghamitra would fully help her father in the construction work. Whenever the father looked at the face of his beloved *Duhita*, he was astonished. At such a young age, she has given up lavish jewellery. She does not wear silk or brightly coloured clothes, with utmost simplicity, wraps all her hair and keeps it tied on her high forehead. Everything seems so strange. The kings, queens, *vimataye* and princesses roaming all around look at her strangely, but like the enlightened sadhvi, there is always the appearance of a shadow of supernatural peace on her face. All the maidens follow every order of Sanghamitra enchanted. Sanghamitra looks like a form of supernatural power in a living woman. She does not interfere in any work of the state, governance and administration. She efficiently handles the task of spreading only the teaching of the Buddha and the word of

Dharma. On the other hand, his beloved brother Mahendra Rajkumar along with his only son Samner has reached Sinhaladweep safely. There the king has given him a grand welcome. The ambassador quickly conveyed this news to the emperor. A huge *Sangh Vihar*has been established there.

This is a beautiful island in the middle of the ocean located in the south of the country of India, where there is an immense wealth of natural treasures with natural beauty. The people of Sihaldweep have faced unrest, chaos and suffering as a result of the fierce battles of their ancestors. Now everyone wants peace in their state. Residents pursuing a simple lifestyle are the exclusive devotees of the present king, if the king has announced to make *Bodh Dharma* the state *dharma*, then there must be an important reason behind it because this is not hypocrisy oriented rather it is an easy, quiet and truth-based teachings about how to live life, that further shows the path of truth. Therefore, the citizens of this place have gathered happily to take initiation. The king himself has requested all the residents of the island to become followers of *Buddhism.* It has become the state religion there. Prince Mahendra initiated hundreds of monks there so that they could enter the Sangha. Not only men, but hundreds of women are also waiting to become nuns. All of them also want to take refuge in Buddha in their lifetime. On the special request of the large public community, the king of Sinhaladweep himself sends special apostles to India. Requests the emperor to send a female bodhisattva imitative, so that she can come and establish a nunnery sangha. On receiving such a special and sweet request, King Chakravarti arranges to send a wise woman. Then Sanghamitra herself appears before her father and humbly prays, "I should be sent to Sinhaladweep for this work, I will establish the Bhikkhuni Sangha and look after it there." Hearing this word from the mouth of her Duhita, the king becomes sad. In any circumstances, he does not want to send his beloved daughter away from him, but Sanghamitra explains to him, "*Nav-Nirvana* will be attained only by following the path of truth for human welfare. Don't be so infatuated with your child. Otherwise, you will deviate from your goal." The father is reassured after listening to the daughter, he realizes that it is not appropriate to obstruct the daughter's path of truth. He allows her to leave. But how can Sanghamitra move away from the shadow of her Bodhi tree, from the touch of it? That tree is the source of her religious consciousness. She requests her father, that she will take a branch of the tree along with her to that island so that all the islanders can see the tree of Bodhigyaan even while staying there. An agricultural specialist was called immediately. He was told to cut the right branch of the Bodhi tree in such a way that it can be shifted to another land. This work took a full month. The branch touching the root of the Bodhi tree was marked. Then in a special style by breaking it from the knot, connecting it with the other original root, tied with the *sutradhars*, keeping it at a particular temperature, it was extended and after a month from the same knot on the right side i.e. in the direction of sunrise towards the east an independent new branch came out blooming on its root. Then it was separated from the original tree, wrapped in the sacred soil of Buddhist Gaya and installed in an urn made of *ashtdhatu* and was presented to be taken to Sinhaladweep.

Sanghamitra accepted that Kalash with great reverence, and after bidding farewell to her parents and the people of the state, she set out on a new journey of her life. She has seen only eighteen *sawans*. She herself has become a nun. During the journey, the king has sent countless servants and servants along, but wearing a rag, an alms pot and an urn of a Bodhi tree plant, Sanghamitra left. She reached Tamaliti from Gaya via Pataliputra. The route of the whole journey is good at some places and rocky at some places. There are inaccessible hills, and somewhere there are thorny bushes. Sanghamitra reached Jabukola port. There, a huge ship was arranged for her and her servants. Sanghamitra has travelled many times with her parents since childhood, but she is taking a sea voyage for the first time. Big waves rising in the sea and salty sea winds are making everyone anxious, but even in those salty winds and the storm that comes in between, she sits very carefully holding the branch of the bodhi tree planted in the vase, as if some mother faces every crisis boldly while protecting her only child from the wrath of nature. In the end, they reach the port of Sihaldweep after passing a difficult long journey of two months. Sanghamitra plants a branch of that sacred Bodhi tree in the ground in the presence of thousands of followers with chanting at the holy site in the eastern corner of the city. The surrounding environment becomes enlightened. The people became overwhelmed and started bowing down to Sanghamitra *Bhikkhuni*. Due to her grace, all the residents of Sinhaladweep present today were blessed. They felt as if Tathagata himself was sitting in a meditative posture under the Bodhi tree.

It was a full moon night of *Paush* month, it seems that night, the moon will soak Anuradhapur with its light. Throughout the day all the nuns are waiting impatiently to take *pravjaya*. In the brightness of the day, everyone saw the method of planting the *Bodhi* tree. Everyone is looking at Sanghamitra with respect. The daughter of such a great *Chakravarti* emperor, showing fearless courage and reverence at such a young age, has come herself to give *pravjaya* to the nuns after travelling such a long journey. The real proof and symbol of women's empowerment is Sanghamitra. Everyone took a bath, cut their hair, put on white clothes and appeared clean in front of the *vihara*. The first nuns' union was established. The king has already built a huge *vihara*. Now only nuns have to take *pravjaya*. Sanghamitra first gave *Pravjaya* to Anula and after that, she started giving *pravjaya* to hundreds of women present there. Sanghamitra now wants to reside here. Gradually, the branches of the *Bodhi* tree started growing there and along with it the number of nuns in the *Sangh* also started increasing. Now Sanghamitra is known here as the first *Aharta Theri*. Her every breath is associated with the air given by the Bodhi tree. She spends the eight *prahars* of the day only in the service of "*Dharma*". Now, this Sinhaladweep is her land of religion, land of knowledge and land of action. For the rest of her life, she remains absorbed only in "*Dharma Darshan*". Before her nirvana, the bhikkhuni tells the *Sangha*, "Keep my *samadhi* in front of the Bodhi tree, from where she sees me and I have her daily darshan. "At the age of eighteen, she attained nirvana, but even today she is sleeping under the shade of the *Bodhi* tree, she is alive, the philosophy of her life is – "*Dharma Darshan*".

❑

Kung's Mother

Tshang has been very disturbed since this morning. The ruler whose kingdom is running in the country. He is, by the way, the government teacher of the state. His grandfather has also been working in the state administration, but now there is an atmosphere of anarchy all around regarding policy, ideas, religion etc. In the palace, the ministers and the royal courtiers of other dynasties are being turmoiled in a very secretive manner. It is no longer appropriate to reside in the capital. Therefore, along with his wife tying a small amount of money, he went to his native state, Pinyang. There he built a small house with his brothers in the village of his ancestors "Wu-wang". His wife Heeka is very beautiful and simple by nature. The couple had been followers of *Confucius* from the very beginning. Social lifestyle is naturally sound and the family practices welfare. Both of them are not ambitious. Cultivating paddy and providing education to the children of the village during the holidays, is their daily routine. The family is the most important unit in the social structure and the birth of a child is considered to be the most important and the source of joy in the family. When Heeka became pregnant, her mother-in-law and other women in the family were overjoyed. She also started dreaming of her to be born child every day. She had the full support of her entire family. The husband is mostly engaged in study mode.

The Saang Raja has ordered the adoption of a new sign language style a few years ago. He is seriously working on the same language style. With the blessings of the gurus, Heeka gets a son*ratna*. A very beautiful child with a round face like the moon, his lips like petals of red lotus and round eyes like diamond pearls, what more does a mother want? A chubby blond boy likes a cotton ball and that too a son. The first son has a special place in society, he is considered very respectable. Heeka's daily routine changed after getting her son. Just as the earth revolves around the sun non-stop, her son is also the centre of her life and twenty-four hours of the day are spent in his upbringing, but the mother, entangled in the web of attachment, forgets that every living being has limited breaths. When her son starts taking food other than his mother's milk, his milk teeth are just about to grow, he chews her breast vigorously while drinking his mother's milk, the mother accepts with great patience and joy, such excruciating pain. She was waiting when her little boy will take out his pearl-like teeth and by consuming food he will become a giant warrior, but before seeing that day, one day the goddess of death embraces him while the child is sleeping. With the death of the first child, both parents almost go mad. The father takes care of himself, but the mother's lament keeps resonating far and wide in the hills. She does not want to give the body of her little child to anyone, but according to the custom, the dead child has to be taken away from her so that his last rites can be performed. For many months there is an atmosphere of sadness and sorrow in the family. Humans are also very optimistic. The couple tries again for their lineage and worships their ancestors so that they may bless them with children. Again, the wife gives birth to another child but this time she is very cautious. From conception to the painful process of delivery, she takes care of her food and medicine with utmost care. She does not let her second beautiful child go outside to anyone. How many times her husband explains that "the outside air and sun rays are much needed for a new born baby. Take the beloved child outside for a while." But the mother ignores her husband's words due to her motherly affection. Time progresses slowly and this little boy is also a victim of Mahakal's feast before even his milk teeth grow. This time a wave of sorrow flows in the whole family. An unconscious mother does not want to come to her senses. In a semi-conscious state, she lies hungry and thirsty, remembering her children throughout the day. Time heals the biggest wounds; many years pass by like this. Seeing the little children of her brother-in-law and relatives laughing and playing, hope starts sprouting in her mind to accept motherhood again. The Jin dynasty is now ruling the state. One day Emperor Mintego has a vision of a grand, radiant, golden man. The emperor sees in a dream that the great man is walking in the sky around his palace. The emperor asks the secret of this dream from his ministers, priests and oceanographers. Everyone tells him that he is the great man Lord Buddha who had preached religion in the country of India, there are followers of Buddhism in many republics in the country of China too. Mintego Emperor is deeply influenced by the teachings of Buddha. Immediately got the "Sangharam Chowk Lan" was constructed so that the Buddha monks, *Ahartas* can come there and propagate the teaching of Buddha and they can migrate. Gradually, the subjects of the state, taking advantage of the teachings of

Buddha, started adopting the same in their lifestyle. At the age of thirty-five, the mother gives birth to a third child. Now her body has become weak. The labour pains have made her more jaded. Her maids are also very frightened because they know about the demise of the two previous children. They know how mentally insecure this woman must be feeling for her child in the maternity home. Be that as it may, when the third son started crying for the first time, the mother forgot the loss of both her children, as if a new life had arisen in her weak body. Don't know from where did so much energy come. The mother was now sure about her third child. *Vaidya* has come and said that this is the last remaining child of the wife because there is no more strength in her body. The next child could be fatal for her. Father has more sympathy for his wife than love, he is satisfied with only one child. He thanks God and ancestors that at least he could become the father of a son. Repeatedly he explains to his wife - "Dear, do not keep ill-will in your mind, nor imagine any bad thing, as we think, it happens, only by wishing good luck to your son, nurture him". This time the wife's mind has become somewhat stable. She has suffered many sorrows in her life. Now, she keeps on doing charity, so that nothing bad happens to her son, but destiny plays its game. Just like the sons before, even before tasting the grain, the third son also closes his eyes. This time the mother has become a stone. Not a drop of tear falls from her eyes in the separation of the son, she keeps gazing at an invisible direction in silence. When the relatives came, when they left with the child's body, she does not know anything. Seeing this condition of her, the maids, sisters-in-law and sister concern all start crying, trying unsuccessfully to make her cry, but the mother has now become a stone.

Now her husband takes care of her more than before, he has stopped teaching work. Those who believe in karma, followers of the policies of *Confucius* their self-confidence have been shattered. Even in mature age, he looks like an old man. On the other hand, it is being discussed in the village that a great monk is staying in Sangharam. He is *trikaldarshi*. A propagator and a preacher. By taking refuge in him, all sorrows are destroyed. The mother also comes to know about this news. She gets impatient after hearing it and tells her husband - "Know about our children, in what form, where they are born, I want to know about my children. Are milking babies born again? I beg at your feet, please find out and come. The husband starts looking at the wife in sorrow. He does not believe in astrology in the slightest, but seeing his wife crying after many years, his heart melts. Sangharam Vihar is very far away. Even though there is no means of transport, the wife is eager to see the monk with her husband. Together they reach the monastery after five days, crossing the inaccessible road. Seeing the peaceful atmosphere there, the young boys taking Buddhist education, all the tiredness of the couple vanishes. After taking bath, they see the monk. The monk blesses them sitting in a calm posture. On one side, in the adjoining seat, a monk-like teacher is sitting. He smiles softly and asks - "you have come to Bhikkhu Sangha from so far, even took blessings, what will you give in alms?" The mother cries and says "I have nothing to give, I have lost my three sons, my lap is empty, I have no support, what can I give you." After a while, she said again - "The most valuable thing of a mother is her child, but I do not even have that, what can I give you."

Guruacharya said - "If you have children, will you donate to the Sangh?" "You don't test me. If I have a child and if he survives, I will give him in the shelter of the Sangh." Then the guru said, "Your child will live for ages. His speech, writing and words will live on in every age." The husband hurtfully looked at the *Bhikku* and said "There are no children here and you are prophesying for ages and ages. My wife is already living in severe pain. We are householders, not renouncers like you, please don't confuse us. Monk smiled calmly and said, "Come in the shelter of Buddha. Everyone will be blessed." After saying this, he got up from the auditorium and went to his room.

The mother came with her husband to her residence with a ray of new hope in her mind. Is this a miracle or a pastime of nature, she conceived again but the doctor and the father are very worried this time. Her physical and mental condition is not suitable for conceiving. Abortion is considered a great sin. That's why they started waiting for the time. Exactly on the ninth day of the ninth month, after severe labour pain, as expected, the child was born from a filthy, weak, sickly-like moon on the *Dwadashi* of *Krishna Paksha*. The maidservants have not even cut the navel cord from the mother. In the same way, the mother hurriedly grabbed the skinny boy with the thin bones of a bird, drenched in dirty blood. After many difficulties and requests, the maids rescued him from the mother, washed him, wrapped him in a cotton cloth and made him sleep again with the mother. Now the mother does not keep him on earth even for a moment. Always keeps him clenched to her chest. It also causes discomfort to the child in breathing, but she is fully presented to save him from the claws of time like a mother. After completing breastfeeding, the child has started consuming some food. Milk teeth have also come out. Mother named him Kung. Kung is attached to the mother's body every moment.

Like they are not two but one life. The beats of the heart also happen simultaneously. The way a monkey walks by sticking its child to the stomach, it does all the work. Kung's mother also keeps him attached to her. Doesn't even allow him to rest his foot on the earth. Kung has never seen sunrise or sunset. He does not know what is the river, mountain, forest, valley or route, he has not gone to the village limits. His mother did not even let him go out of his room. His teeth have now come out like pearls. But the mother does not allow even the sun's rays to fall on him. Doesn't even allow breathing in the pure air outside. Every moment the child moves around in the lap, due to which the child has neither learned to sit properly nor walk, he is always sick and tired. *Vaidya* and his father explain many times that let the child grow in the lap of nature only, then only his proper development will take place, but Mohini the mother does not listen to anyone. When the child turns five years old, he fell seriously ill. Herbal juices and medicines are not working on him, then the wise man of the village said - "You had to donate it in alms, go to the monastery and donate it to the monk. He is theirs and will be safe near them". The mother remembered the words given by her. She kept staring at her child all night, after drinking all the sorrows in the morning and giving the stars of her eyes to her husband, she said – "Go take him to the refuge of Buddha. If he survives by keeping him away from my eyes, then I accept the separation of my son. With a heavy heart, the father gives his son to the monastery. When the father reaches there, the sound of the mantra is heard in his ears -

"Buddha sharanam gacchami, dhamma sharanam gacchami, sangham sharanam gachhami."

Hearing this sound, the disturbed father's mind

becomes completely calm. The dying little Kung starts to move in his lap.

The monk comes and takes him out of his father's lap with great affection and holds him by the hand and takes him to the chief monk of Sangharam Vihara. Kung has set foot on earth for the first time. At first, he stumbled, then holding the monk's hand, slowly started moving forward. For the first time, he saw a huge sky above, turned his gaze around and saw the calm monks wearing *chevre* walking, *Son Chiraya* (bird) is chirping sitting on the branch of the tree. The faint rays of the sun are falling on him playing hide and seek amidst the clouds. Pure air is flowing through his nostrils and reaching his weak lungs, transmitting power. The father returned to the village rest assured, but the mother's mind is sad. Kung has started recovering very quickly in SangharamVihar. He runs in the path of the valleys like a leopard. The body has also become well-formed. Completes all the work of Vihar with utmost efficiency. His great-grandfather was a government official in the state, his father was a teacher, these qualities have been inherited by him. He always succeeds in the study of Buddhist education. Then the youths who received education in the viharas had to work in the paddy fields like the *"Samaners"*. Kung also cultivates paddy in the fields but at other times he only takes the teachings of Buddha. Once some youths, both due to poverty and lack of food, come to steal the harvested paddy in his fields, seeing that they have weapons in their hands, Kung and the fellow disciples of Buddha run away and hide, but Kung gives them a huge roar and says, "Go take all this harvested paddy. You people did not know how many sins you had committed in your previous lives, now you are stealing and getting food. Think for how many more lives you have to commit sins to be free from the sin of theft of this birth, then you will never be free." Saying this he gave all the paddy to him. Hearing his words, the youths who came to steal were so impressed that they felt very pity on their condition and by holding his feet, they started apologizing and came to the monastery and became a follower of Buddhism. After this incident, Kung received *Pravajya*. Now he devotes all his time to the teachings of Buddhism and writing scriptures. Meanwhile, the mother sends him a message that his father has passed away. Being a son, he has to come to the village.

Kung replies to his uncle – "I am a monk over here. I want to get rid of the cycle of birth and death. The pleasures of a householder's life do not attract me, death does not cause sorrow and my life is devoted to education, teaching and truth. Please don't request me to go to the village." His uncle was surprised to hear the voice of Kishore Kung, who spoke of so much knowledge at such a young age. After returning home, he gave the details of his conversation to Kung's mother. Mother's heart was disturbed that the only living son is not coming to visit his dead father, but somewhere in the corner of her heart, a ray of hope is burning that her son is trying for society. His only surviving child will live forever, but how? This question still haunts Kung's mother. She welcomes the prophecy that he will live for ages, but the news also comes to an ordinary mother after a while that Kung has now become a full-fledged monk. He is the best teacher. People from all over the state of China come to listen to his teachings. The son who was not allowed to set foot on the earth for five years, Kung today travels around the world. Sharing the knowledge of Buddha. He wants to discover the *"Vinayasutra"* of the *"Tripitaka"* of Budha education. He wants to go to the birthplace of Gautam Buddha, he wants to go to the place where Tathagata had attained "divine knowledge", and he wants to visit every path where Bhante himself had walked. But he does not want to read the feelings of the old widowed mother's heart, does not want to flow in the love flowing from the mother's heart. If Kung is bound by maternal attachment, then he will only remain her son, but if he will work for the *Dhamma* he will be remembered for ages. Now Kung has also become a teacher. He has been adorned by the emperor with the title of *"Fahian"*. "Fa" means *Dharma*, and *"Hyan"* means Acharya Guru, that is, the master of *Dhamma*. Now the scripted speech of *"Fahian"* the budha's words is being written in the sign state language of China. Kung also wants to come to the land of India and study the special holy Buddhist texts and translate them into his mother tongue, but there is a weak cord of love which is still invisibly tying Kung to his mother. The recluse, even after being a past-goer, has not yet become completely independent. Kung's mother does not want to hinder his life's journey. She remembers *Tathagata* in her mind, prays him to free her from this life. Kung gets the news of his mother's death. Feels a little something somewhere in the heart but he is a monk and shedding tears on the death of loved ones is a crime. He is beyond the feelings like happiness and sorrow. Kung's tears do not come out. Though they do not come out of the eyes, gets absorbed peacefully in the heart itself, but once he goes to his birthplace to have the last glimpse of his mother. The whole village is waiting for him. Fulfilling the last wish of his biological mother, he goes to visit her tomb. All the villagers are amazed to see him as a monk and everyone bows to him with reverence. Fahien has forever severed his ties with the weak cord inside his mind. Now that he is completely free, he has yet to do great things. To travel abroad, to write the description of trips and to translate Buddhist texts. Kung's mother is now rested and freed from the cycle of life and death. No one takes his name in history, but the fourth child to whom she gave birth by betting her life, he is still remembered in the form of a preacher, eminent history writer, *Yayavar*, Buddhist teacher, first Chinese traveller, Buddhist *Dhamma* text translator, the thinker is alive in the world.

❑

Black Eagle Books

www.blackeaglebooks.org
info@blackeaglebooks.org

Black Eagle Books, an independent publisher, was founded as a nonprofit organization in April, 2019. It is our mission to connect and engage the Indian diaspora and the world at large with the best of works of world literature published on a collaborative platform, with special emphasis on foregrounding Contemporary Classics and New Writing.